TABLE OF CONTENTS

By J.E. Clarkson

THE VANISHING OFFICE.

By J.E. Clarkson

Dedications.
For my wonderful partner Anton, my family and best friends Jacky, who doggedly proofread each chapter and Jossy, who always encouraged me. I couldn't have written this book without you all.

Forward.

The keyboards clicked and clacked like the inner workings of a clock. Many clocks, in fact as rows upon rows of expressionless workers typed up information, then changed it. This room did not exist, inside a building that did not exist. The workers did exist but their identities were the first bits of information that were changed. They had been recruited from all walks of life, using that most banal of recruitment measures, the online CV.

Your background wasn't important. There was many a fire-fighter's daughter or an estate agent's son. Dustman or Duke, it really didn't matter. The only thing that did, was absolute allegiance and unquestioning loyalty. It was also vital to to be able to perform quite mind-bending feats of self-delusion and self-justification, the ability to ignore whatever you were typing in, however heinous or distressing and merely type out what was required. Unquestioningly. Being enormously deceitful was also of great benefit as was having the ability to tell a good story.

It was not possible to work there if you were ever even slightly bothered by the drip,drip,drip of your conscience. That was fatal. Often metaphorically, sometimes literally. There were times when I looked across at those neat rows of humanity and noticed a gap in the line. Like Morse code.

How did I know all of this? To them, I was as invisible as the room and the building itself. I simply didn't exist. But whether I existed to them or not, didn't matter. I was taking notes and they did exist.

CHAPTER 1

Day 1

The day broke sharp. The nagging bleeps of my digital alarm combined with the offensive time, caused a raging tension headache. Waking up during the blue hour is not something I would've gladly chosen to do. I'm not a lark. I trudged downstairs cradling a large cup of coffee and peered through the curtains and down on to the street below. It was mainly empty but one or two workers buzzed around making their way into the centre of the city. Very few carried brief cases. Some wore fluorescent jackets. Most looked at the floor and tried to avoid the few other people around them. It was my first day. I wondered what would face me once I arrived at the office. I hadn't expected to get a job so quickly and it almost seemed too good to be true. No interview was necessary which I found a bit odd but didn't question it at the time. I needed the money. Keeping the door shut to stop the bailiffs loses its charm very quickly.

I was head hunted online. The original e-mail reminded me of those cards you used to find in phone boxes. It was strangely seductive but not very subtle at all. It was a bit like being clubbed over the head.

"Short on cash? We need cleaners for our city centre office. You have met the criteria. No experience required as full training will be given. Generous pay as unsocial hours a certainty. Confidentiality essential."

I wondered about the secrecy of what I was about to become involved in. How many secrets could you be exposed to as a cleaner anyway? I was about to find out.

****

The buzzer was unobtrusive, I almost missed it. After I pressed it, no one answered, the door just opened inwardly. How do they know it's me, I wondered? I then saw the small camera above the door. They already have my photo, I thought and found it rather creepy as I hadn't given them it. They must have found it online.

I walked down a very narrow, dark corridor. It funnelled me in one direction only. Straight ahead. Once I reached the end, I noticed a brilliant blue light fixed to the right-hand wall. It illuminated a sliding door made of polished metal. I couldn't work out what metal it was but it looked brutal and unbending.

As I reached the door, I couldn't see any obvious way through it. No buttons, door knobs or handles.

A metallic voice rang out.

"I'll let you in." It said.

The door opened of its own accord. I walked through and into a cavernous room filled with row upon row of desks and chairs. Upon each desk was an identical laptop. They looked up to date and expensive. There was also a light and headset but nothing else. No photos or plants. It wasn't cosy at all. There was also no natural light at all or windows. I thought it was on street level but wasn't sure. It felt like an underground bunker but it didn't feel like I'd walked down any slopes. It was very disorienting.

" You'd better collect your cleaning equipment." The voice rang out again.

" You've only got a couple of hours before the other workers get here"

"Where is my equipment?" I asked as it wasn't obvious where it was.

" The trolley in the corner. It's yellow. You can't miss it." The voice said.

A spotlight appeared in the far-left hand corner of the room. It was highlighting a yellow cleaning trolley. I knew it hadn't been there when I first entered the room. Someone else had put it there, but I hadn't heard or seen anyone. It had been completely silent with the exception of a very low buzzing that reminded me of a dying bathroom light. You could go mad in a place like that, if you stayed there long enough. I made my way towards the trolley, picked up a spray and put my gloves on.

****

"You have 10 minutes before the office is full." The voice said.

I still had around ten desks to clean.

"Do I have to be finished before then?" I said

"No but when the alarm goes off you must leave immediately."

"Ok." I replied.

I wondered what kind of office needed an alarm. It was very strange in the same way that most things that had happened since I entered the building were strange.

I ended up finishing more quickly than expected and so the workers all filed in just as I was finishing up. No one looked at or acknowledged me at all, but they also didn't talk or look at each other either. It was as if each person were in their own bubble, separated by a skin of silence.

I looked at the floor fearing the consequence of looking at the other workers as they filed in. I clumsily knocked into a pale man and apologised. He looked at me in a strange way but apart from that he didn't react at all. I was like a ghost who'd walked through a wall.

****

After such a weird morning, I was glad to get home and as I started so early, it meant I had the afternoon free. I was exhausted, not being used to getting up so early. So, I laid down on the bed and got ready to snooze for a few hours. As my eyes were getting heavy, I heard my mobile ping. I quickly checked it to see who was messaging.

It was an anonymous number and I was almost ready to delete the message but curiosity got the better of me.

"Your first wages, £300. You did a good job and have passed the trial period. From tomorrow, you will receive £750 a week which will go up to £1,000 after 3 months. You must arrive at 4 O' clock sharp for the 3 mornings worked. Sometimes you will not finish your shift but you will be paid as if you had. Your shift will usually be 5 hours. Sometimes you will be called in on your days off. You cannot refuse as this will terminate your contract but you will be paid double. You cannot discuss anything you see or hear or this will terminate your contract. You cannot join a union or this will terminate your contract. If you have any problems discuss it with Stella when you arrive at work, anything reasonable she can sort out for you. These are your terms and conditions. They are non-negotiable. Do you accept?"

My first thought was that so much of the message was ridiculous. The amounts of money involved, the rigidity of the conditions. It didn't even sound legal but the money swung it. But not being completely naive, I thought it would be a good idea to check my bank balance.

As the message said, £300 had been paid in. By Nemo And Co. It all looked above board, yet I still felt nervous about it.

You don't have to do this forever, I thought, suppressing any doubts.

Before I fell asleep, I sent a single word message in reply.

"Yes."

****

"Bit unusual you paying for drinks? You won the lottery?" Ellen said. I knew it wasn't something I'd done for a while. I couldn't afford to.

"Well, I've been paid so thought it was about time."

"I like this new job." Said Ellen.

"It's nice having some more money for a change, that's for sure." I smiled while taking a swig of white wine.

I looked around at the bar. It was our local and had been for years. Not a glamorous or trendy place, it was filled with threadbare ancient settees. Many of the clientele were almost as threadbare themselves. It was only possible to see silhouettes. Half-faces, dimly lit by standard lamps. Some were drinking and laughing, others eating and flirting and some studiously ignoring those they were drinking with, as they stared glumly at the bottom of their glass. I sensed the eerie sensation of being watched but in the absence of bright light, had no idea by whom.

"Ellen you ready to leave?" I asked.

"What? Already?" Ellen made a face.

" Yes, I've got an early start." I replied.

I looked around seeing if it was possible to work out if anyone was watching or if I was just being paranoid. In the gloom, I could see the glint of one of the standard lamps reflected on a pair of spectacles. They were looking straight at me but I couldn't see the eyes behind them.

"Ellen come on." I growled through gritted teeth. I grabbed Ellen's arm and pulled her out of the door. If I'd left slightly more slowly, I might have noticed the owner of the spectacles raising their glass.

****

To be at the office for 4 O'clock. I needed to get up at half past two. Thankfully we arrived back at the flat by half past nine. Ellen grumbled for about half an hour until the Chinese take away arrived, also paid for by me then, she happily watched DVDs until she crashed out on the settee. I ended up curled up in bed by half past ten but couldn't sleep. I had a growing sense of unease about being watched. Had I imagined it? Ellen hadn't noticed anything either in the pub or on the way home, but I couldn't shake it off.

Things just kept going round and round in my mind. The weird set up in the office. The money message and the strange surveillance in the pub. I was beginning to wonder if I had imagined it all or at least, exaggerated it. Looking at the red digits on the alarm clock, I knew I needed to sleep as quickly as possible.

Just as my eyes began to close, my phone pinged again.

"Well done for not saying anything." The message read.

CHAPTER 2

Day 2

The cold buzzing of the alarm woke me. It felt like I'd only been asleep for two minutes. Grabbing an enormous mug of coffee, I sat on an armchair and watched Ellen as she drooled and snored quietly. What to make of the late-night message?

I'd obviously been right that we were being watched in the pub. Had we been followed to the flat? I'd not noticed anyone behind us but then that was the point. To be anonymous and unnoticeable. I had a quick look out of the window. What was I expecting? Some guy in a trilby and dark glasses, speaking into his collar.

"Wha...?" Ellen slurred half asleep.

"I'm off to work in a few minutes. Go back to sleep." I said.

"It's still night. Ridiculous." Ellen grumbled away to herself.

"Stop moaning. It'll be nearly evening by the time you get up." I teased.

"Not my fault you've got a stupid job." Ellen said.

"A well-paid stupid job, that paid for your drinks and late-night snacks."

Ellen just grunted and put a pillow over her head. She flipped me the bird as I closed the door behind me.

****

I got to the office at five to four. The journey had been quiet with it still being so early. An invisible city was rising and beavering away, preparing itself for when the other commuters arrived. It was strange being a part of this unnoticed underground that was also often unappreciated. We were the engine room that drove the city.

The door opened inwardly before I even rang the buzzer this time.

The familiar tinny voice rang out.

"You're on time, but only just. A good job all the buses weren't late." A passive aggressive computer, I thought. Just my luck.

I walked down the corridor and to my amazement when the door opened, I saw that all of the desks were filled with workers typing away in silence. I walked through the rows of desks and into the left-hand corner, where the yellow cleaning trolley was waiting for me. I wasn't sure how much cleaning I could do whilst the office was so full. Almost instantaneously a bell rang out and the workers rose from their desks and made their way to the exits. One door being the one I had just come in and another which seemed invisible in the furthest right-hand corner of the room. I wasn't sure whether this was the alarm that had been mentioned the day before.

As I stood puzzled by the cleaning trolley, the voice rang out again.

"They've been here all night. The signal isn't for you. Just carry on as usual "

I nodded and went about picking up my cleaning equipment from the trolley. As I turned around, I felt one of the figures bump into me as he walked past. I grimaced slightly. Before I could remonstrate or even see who it was the figure was gone.

I shrugged and began to clean. Looking at my watch, I saw that time was passing quickly. For a third time the voice spoke.

"Come on hurry. The next shift will be here in four hours. You'll need to be finished by then."

I nodded and set to work. It was a good job the money was decent and I was so glad that I wouldn't be working the next day. I had calculated that if I could stick the early hours and the digital dictator, I could leave the job within 6 months and not have to work for at least a year. A year to write and not have to worry. I had to do it.

****

Four and a half hours later, sitting on the 45 bus, I was nodding forward. Hard. I was so tired; I hadn't noticed another passenger sit down next to me. They said nothing but I could feel their eyes scrutinizing me.

I opened one eye and then the other and looked into a familiar face that I couldn't quite place. It made me jump. They were staring right into my eyes. They leaned over and said.

"Check your pocket."

With that, they got up and pressed the bell for the next bus stop. I watched them as they descended the stairs. They didn't look back. What had just happened? I tried to remember the face and where I knew it from. He was a pallid, nondescript man with light blonde, slicked back hair. I tried to rack my brains as I rummaged in my pocket. Inside was a tiny, folded piece of paper. I opened it, apprehensive about what it might say. There was only one word in faded typescript, barely legible.

"Help".

****

I lost count of the number of times I turned around to see if I was being followed on the walk home. I couldn't see anyone but that didn't mean that they weren't there, watching. I wondered if Ellen was still there or if she'd pulled a sickie. She was lucky that her boss was fairly laid back and so she could get away with it. I didn't know if it was better that she was there or not.

I really wanted to talk to her about everything but had a sinking feeling. Somehow, someone had me under surveillance, that was obvious from the messages that I'd got. But more than that, whoever they were, they were always one step ahead of me and I didn't know how. I wasn't sure that it was a good idea for Ellen to be there when I got back. For her or me.

Walking into the lounge, my heart sank. There she was sprawled out on the settee still sleeping. I exhaled deeply and went into the bedroom.

What to do with the letter? It was obviously important but why had they chosen me and what could I do about it anyway? I decided to keep it locked away in my jewellery box. It annoyed me that I knew the man who had given me it but couldn't place him.

As I drew the blind, there was a little tap at the door. Ellen peered around it.

" Are you awake still? " She asked.

" Just about." I replied.

" There's been a bomb on a bus."

" Oh hell. Which one?"

"75. It's on the news now."

I turned the bedroom tv on and Ellen and I sat huddled together on the bed as we watched. The bus looked mainly unscathed apart from a square shaped hole at the back of the top deck. That part of the roof appeared to arch away from the main body of the bus. It looked like a half-opened mackerel tin.

" Bloody hell. I hope there weren't many people on the top deck. Rush hour and all that." Said Ellen.

I just nodded and stayed glued to the screen as the camera panned around to the front.

" Oh, that's weird." I said.

" What is?" Ellen replied.

" Look at what it says on the front." I said.

" Yes, number 75, so what?" Said Ellen.

" Come on, Sherlock. Look again." I urged.

Ellen looked puzzled for a few seconds as she squinted at the screen then it dawned on her.

"Not in service? Why the hell would anyone bomb an empty bus that wasn't in service?" She asked.

"Exactly. Why indeed?" I replied.

****

When I woke up hours later it was dark. Ellen had gone. I looked at the clock. It was 10 o'clock. Good job I'm off tomorrow, I thought but then my next thought was that it might be a good idea to double check I hadn't been sent a message from the office to come in. There was an unopened text and my heart sank a little bit.

"Thank you for today. Don't worry, you're still off tomorrow."

My heart leapt a bit in relief. The text continued.

"You may have seen in the news about the bus bombing. Unfortunately, a worker from the office was killed in it. It will be common knowledge as the police will be publishing their picture in the media by this evening. We would ask that you do not share this information with anyone. If you do, your contract will be terminated. We have deposited another three hundred pounds in your bank to aid you in this decision. It will be documented as expenses. Once you have read this message, we would ask that you delete it. Thank you for your cooperation."

The text was signed off by Stella.

I took a deep breath and had a look to see what time the text had been sent.

Nine O'clock. One hour ago. I didn't know what to make of it. I went into the kitchen to make a coffee. There was no sign of Ellen. It seemed like she'd gone home. I texted her to make sure she'd got back ok and turned the tv back on.

"Police sources are telling us that two people were killed in the bombing of bus number 75. This is yet to be confirmed officially but questions are bound to be asked why an out of service bus was carrying two passengers at all?" The newsreader droned solemnly.

I suddenly felt cold. Why was an employee of Nemo and Co. on an out of service bus at all? And more to the point, why had the bus been bombed? I looked again at the message from Stella. I had so many questions. They were bouncing around my brain like bullets. Why send me the text at all? I didn't know any of the other employees, we weren't colleagues or friends. It seemed to me that we were actively encouraged to avoid each other, so why burden me with this knowledge that I was under pressure to keep secret? None of it made any sense at all.

I watched the screen with a sense of numbness. I couldn't take anything in. The information scrolling across the bottom was a word salad. It wouldn't compute. The doorbell rang. Maybe it was Ellen? But normally she would ring or text ahead.

"Hello?" I answered.

"Food delivery." A male voice said.

"But I didn't order anything." I replied.

"Sent from a friend." They replied.

I wondered if Ellen had felt bad and wanted to repay me for the treats from the night before.

I sent a text thanking her then went downstairs to pick up the delivery.

I opened the door and saw a man standing there, a pair of square glasses peeking out from under his baseball cap. He smiled and I noticed a couple of gold teeth glinting under the gaze of the streetlight. I thanked him and went upstairs. Just as I placed the bag on the kitchen table, my phone pinged again. It was from Ellen.

"Home safe. Take away not from me. Have you got a secret admirer? Lucky sod. Hugs."

I rifled through the bag and placed the containers on the table. Prawn toasts, beef in oyster sauce and special fried rice. At the bottom of the bag, I found a typed note.

" Thanks for all the good work so far. Hope I got the order right. Regards, Stella."

****

CHAPTER 3

The walk to the Internet cafe was quiet and the pools of light made by the lampposts seemed like islands of safety in the dark pavement. It had been a long time since I'd been there but Stella seemed to know an unnerving amount about my private life and I didn't know how. The takeaway was nice, delicious in fact, but it had the feeling of obligation about it.

I made sure to walk a couple of times around the block and wore a hat pulled down over my face and loose clothing in case I was being followed. I also left my phone at home switched off. Ellen would be having a field day if she saw me right now, I thought. But I wanted to find out more about Nemo and Co. and didn't feel I could do it from home.

After doing a number of circuits around the block and not noticing anyone following, I wandered into the Internet cafe and ordered a large Americano, then sat down at a computer terminal. I wasn't sure what I was looking for to begin with. I just typed Nemo and Co. to see what would come up.

There were a few lines about it on the companies' house page but it appeared, to all intents and purposes, to be a shell company. The address was the same as the building I worked in, 19 c Black Swan Mews. The only information about what the company actually did was an article hidden away on a business page. It mentioned data processing and a few lines about the amount of profit that the company had made. The amount was listed as substantially less on the companies' house page than in the article, but that didn't strike me as particularly unusual. Companies often seemed to underreport profits but what really interested me was the data processing. Whose data did they process and how was it so profitable? I didn't believe the companies house profit declaration for one minute, it seemed pretty likely that that was some kind of tax avoidance strategy.

I wanted to keep some kind of record but didn't think it was wise to save any documents on a memory stick. I looked in my bag and found an eye liner and old serviette then scrawled down whatever I could then stuffed the scruffy piece of paper back into my pocket with my keys. I looked at my watch. Midnight, it was really time to be getting back. I nipped into the toilet and as left, I looked up at the cafe owner to say thanks and goodnight but they were talking on the phone. I didn't think they had even noticed me leaving.

Fairly quickly after I left the internet cafe, I could hear footsteps behind me. I turned around but couldn't see anyone. Nevertheless, it made me feel nervous and so I speeded up. Those pools of lamplight no longer seemed comforting. Now, they were prison searchlights looking to round up escapees. As I ran between the lampposts, the following footsteps grew louder and closer. I soon felt something cold and sharp pointing into my neck.

" Give me your bag. "A voice whispered.

I didn't even think about protesting and handed it over. I was both glad and simultaneously regretting the fact that my phone was at home. I hoped that there wouldn't be two dead Nemo and Co. employees in two days. If I was murdered, would Stella be sending messages to other people telling them to keep my murder secret? I doubted it only being the office cleaner, but who the hell knew. The figure withdrew their knife from my neck and ran off into the night.

"Are you OK?"

Another figure held out a hand and helped me up. A halo of light shone behind them. I couldn't see their eyes just a glinting of gold teeth. I shivered.

" Let me order you a taxi. You've had a shock."

I noticed the faintest hint of a cockney accent but it almost seemed as if it was put on. It was just that little bit too strong so it didn't ring true. Still, it was very kind of him to order me a cab even though I only lived around the corner. He sat me down on a shop door step and for a second, I wondered if I was being just a little bit too trusting but he gave me plenty of space and soon enough, the taxi arrived. He opened the door for me and then closed it once I'd sat down.

"Take care." He said through the taxi window and then disappeared into the night.

"Where to love?" Said the driver.

I smiled as his was a proper cockney accent.

"Oh, just Lyle Street please." I answered.

"Not very far, babe is it?" He said, disappointed.

"No. I just got mugged and someone nicked my bag." I said.

"Oh, what a toe rag. Sorry love." He said and looked at me sympathetically through his rear-view mirror.

"Yes." I then realized my wallet was in my bag. "Oh shit, I don't know how I'm going to pay you." I said.

"Don't worry. The guvnor's sorted it. Tip as well, so it's all good." He laughed.

I was both grateful and confused. Was it all a coincidence? I was on the receiving end of a number of acts of generosity but they seemed to have hooks in. I shook my head. Things were getting so weird that I was getting paranoid. But then, had a boss ever sent a delivery of food round that was already paid for?

I thanked the driver and let myself into the flat. I checked my phone was still on the kitchen table. It was and was blinking with new messages. Six from Ellen, one from Stella and one from another number that I didn't recognize. I opened Ellen's first.

"U ok? Who's the secret admirer? Don't keep me hanging!!! Xx"

Doesn't matter what's going on bus bombings, muggings, World War Three, Ellen must have her gossip, I thought. The next four texts were increasingly frustrated versions of the same text. The final one said.

"Something's not right. Ring me asap."

Was she just being a drama queen as usual? I was beginning to feel anxious. Surely it was just Ellen being impatient. I wanted to convince myself nothing else was wrong but instinctively something felt off. I dialed Ellen's number. There was no answer. I tried again and still nothing. What the hell was going on? I tried for a third time and was interrupted by the doorbell. I hesitated to answer. The doorbell rang again but more insistently this time. I picked up the intercom and mentally practiced my escape in case someone kicked the door in.

"It's me." Ellen bellowed into the intercom.

I buzzed the door to let her in and she flew past me and into the toilet where she spent the next few minutes throwing up. She'd locked the door so I was unable to go in and see how she was. I sat down on the settee and reached into my side pocket. The receipt for the Internet cafe and Americano had gone as had a half-used chap stick. I fished around in my other pocket and found a packet of Extra Strong Mints still there.

At that moment, Ellen appeared in the doorway looking gaunt and shaken. I patted at the seat next to me and put my arm around her shoulders. She lay her head on mine and sobbed uncontrollably.

"What's happened?" I asked.

She looked at me through rivulets of black eyeliner. She was obviously finding it difficult to speak as her breathing juddered loudly in and out. Her shoulders rose and fell rapidly.

"I think I was spiked and I don't know if I was raped." Ellen said.

"Oh bloody hell . Where did this happen ?" I replied

"At some guy's house. I was bored and a bit jealous of your secret admirer so I went on tinder."

"Oh Ellen. I don't have a secret admirer. It was bloody Stella, my new boss from work."

Ellen stopped crying for a moment and looked thoughtful.

"She's not trying it on with you, is she? It does happen across all sexualities. I mean it's OK if that's what you wanted." She said.

"For God's sake, Ellen. I've never even met her. Not once. I just get texts from her about work and hear her voice on the office intercom sometimes. A bit weird but I think it's something to do with all that sort of motivational bullshit. Loads of treats and then you work harder." I said.

A thought crossed my mind, that maybe I shouldn't really be telling Ellen about all of this. Her being vulnerable had made me throw caution to the wind a bit. Maybe this would mean that my contract would be terminated as Stella constantly re-iterated in her texts. I was getting beyond the point of caring. If it happened, it happened. Tonight, we'd been mugged, spiked and possibly raped between us. Whether I kept or lost an admittedly very well-paid cleaning job was of no consequence in the grand scheme of things.

"Ellen have you been to the hospital? Or the police about this yet?" I asked.

Ellen shook her head.

"No. I can't really remember anything and apart from that, I'd had a drink. I'm not sure if anyone would take it seriously."

She started to cry. I grabbed her hand and looked at her.

"Come on we need to go down to the hospital at least and get you checked out."

I opened the blind slightly and looked out of the window. The pale blue light just before dawn filtered through the slats and into the room. The street appeared to be empty. There was even an absence of cars and buses in the road. There was part of me that felt it was just too quiet. There was no peace or tranquility about it. More a tense absence of action that you couldn't see. A bit like a virus bubbling under.

****

CHAPTER 4

Day 3

There's something about accident and emergency. Waiting seems to take forever there. There's often an interesting cast of characters to watch though, and that can break the monotony. It took about three hours for Ellen to be seen and I was sat alone for another hour and a half while she was being assessed. I offered to go in with her but she insisted she wanted to be alone. Ellen was very good at being charming, sparkling and funny but not so good at being vulnerable.

I sat drinking vending machine coffee and watching the hands of the black and white clock moving ever more slowly. Einstein was right, I thought. I looked at the mixture of faces sitting around the waiting room. Worried, bored, some were drunk and others, blank faced and emotionless, pretending they were somewhere else. I felt myself drifting off to sleep and had the sensation that someone was sitting down next to me. I was too tired to open my eyes or trying to make conversation so I pretended to be asleep. I felt them get up again and as they did, they knocked the chair roughly and dropped something on the floor that made a loud bang. I jumped and my eyes snapped open. I looked into the eyes of a very thin woman. She looked haunted and only held eye contact for a few seconds.

"Sorry." She said and then quickly walked off. Irritated by being shaken awake, I was about to remonstrate with her but then noticed the package on the floor. It was an A4 Manila envelope. It was stuffed full of something.

"Wait!" I called after her. "Is this yours?"

The woman turned around to look at me, said nothing and continued to walk off. I picked up the envelope and took a quick look at the outside.

There was no name or address written on either the front or the back. I wondered if it could be important but the woman hadn't seemed overly concerned about losing it, if it was indeed hers.

Ellen appeared around the corner at that moment, looking tearful but slightly more relaxed than she had when we'd arrived.

" They don't think I've been raped but they're fairly sure that I've been spiked. They said that I shouldn't go to work tomorrow or be left alone for 24 hours." She said.

"Well looks like you're coming to stay with me for the day then." I answered.

"What's in the envelope?" Ellen asked.

I looked at it, forgetting that I had it for a few moments.

"I really don't know. Come on let's go back home and we can look at it later once we've had a sleep. "I said

****

It was fully light when we got in. I placed the envelope on my bedside table and then realized in my haste to look after Ellen, I hadn't checked the message from Stella. If my day off had been changed it was too late now. 4 O'clock came and went hours ago. Part of me almost wished that Stella's message was just that and that I'd missed the shift and been sacked. There was something very odd about Nemo and co that I couldn't put my finger on. That combined with my being mugged and Ellen being spiked, I was craving some normality. Even the bailiffs on my doorstep would be preferable at the moment. At least I wouldn't have to let them in.

I opened Stella's message. There was no mention of shifts changing, my heart sank a bit. There was only three words.

" Beware strange women."

What about strange computers, I thought? It was too much drama for one day and so in order to avoid any more obscure messages from Stella, I turned my phone off and left it charging on the kitchen surface. I stuck my head around the lounge door one last time to check on Ellen before I went to bed. She was already asleep on the settee. I was going to offer to give her the bed considering what she'd been through, but didn't want to wake her again. As I got undressed in the bedroom, I found the serviette I'd written the Nemo and co information on, in my shoe. I'd forgotten all about it.

****

CHAPTER 5

His voice rang in my ears. Just one word over and over again. "Help". He'd only said three words to me. Now he was dead. His pale face twisted out of shape like melting plastic but I could see his mouth trying to form other words but he could only keep saying the same thing. Everything went dark. The glass blew outwards and the roof disappeared into the sky. I was bolted to my seat. Debris flew around me in slow motion and I was buffeted by shockwaves that I couldn't avoid. I was going to be eviscerated but the debris kept bouncing off and flying into the void that was increasingly growing around the bus. The man was being dragged backwards by an invisible force and his cold; dead hands kept clawing into the metal floor.

His face kept changing shape in horrifying speed but his mouth continued mouthing the same word over and over. Pieces of ripped paper swirled around picking up speed then funnelling into a tornado shape that at its height swooped over the man and then drew him in. It was as if my eyes were taped open, I couldn't look away as this digesting funnel of pulp, spat out the bones of this poor, wretched man and then fluttered to the floor in a thousand different pieces. Each piece of paper had "help" written on it in black eyeliner. In my handwriting. Then the bus and all of its contents disappeared. There was only me sitting on a seat in the midst of a thick grey fog. In the distance was a very quiet voice being projected through what sounded like a public address system. It was tinny and thin and I couldn't make out what it was saying. I tried to move from the chair but as it was impossible. I was clamped to the seat yet again. I closed my eyes trying to avoid the swirling fog as it stung and made me cough.

I counted to ten and then when I opened my eyes again, the fog had cleared.

The voice on the loud speaker was getting gradually louder. As I looked around, I realized that I was sat in the office surrounded by row upon row of workers. As I turned to look at each worker, I saw that they all had the same face. The face of the dead man on the bus and they were all asking for help. Silently.

I put my hands over my face trying to shut them all out. Then they all simultaneously started typing but they weren't typing on computer keyboards, but on traditional typewriters. The keys clattered and built to a loud crescendo that was broken by a chorus of bells that rang out every time that a typist had reached the end of a sentence. I tried to speak, to shout anything to drown out the noise of the bells and keys but I couldn't make any sound, however hard I tried. I also started to become aware of a quiet whirring sound. It gradually became louder and louder then as it did so, the sound of the typewriter keys and bells grew quieter and quieter until they disappeared completely. I opened my eyes and all of the workers had vanished. I was sat alone in the empty room. The whirring continued to get louder. In the left-hand corner of the room, I could see a metallic figure moving very gradually towards me. It seemed to be walking very deliberately.

As each footstep hit the floor, I could feel vibrations through the desk. There was a humming sense of menace that unfurled across the room as the figure edged closer. I looked up and suddenly there it was, stood facing me across the desk. We both looked at each other, not moving at all.

The figure was humanoid and appeared to be female. Her eyes were black opaque almonds that glinted and reflected the fluorescent lighting on the office ceiling. Her body was slim and wiry, with each muscle defined carefully. She looked like she had been chiselled from chrome in one sitting. With the exception of her eyes, she was unnervingly human looking. Her cheekbones slanted upwards and her lips were closed and un-moving. She had no hair but there was an arc on the top of her head that almost looked like a crown. We continued to look at each other as if sizing up the opposition. She reminded me of an avenging angel, but what terrible crime would you have had to have committed for her to be sent after you as retribution?

As we looked at each other, she began to speak in a metallic, robotic voice.

"Beware strange women, she said, then " If you don't, your contract will be terminated."

Her lips still didn't move. Her voice was merely projected through a digital voice box. I daren't move. I still felt pinned to the chair but no longer knew if it was because of being paralysed by fear. She repeated her warnings but at the same time, she tapped the desk and moved gradually closer. Once again, she repeated her warnings but began to tap more loudly on the desk until her warnings and the tapping became rhythmic drumming, growing louder with each warning. Soon the tapping became banging and as the banging grew louder, she began to circle the desk in grand elliptical sweeps. I could no longer follow her as she was able to move more quickly than my eyes could follow. I closed my eyes but I could still see flashes of chrome swooping around through my eyelids. Then I felt fingers clamped down on my shoulders and I was shaken so hard that I felt my teeth rattle in my mouth.

All I could hear was;

"Your contract will be terminated." Over and over again.

****

" Wake up, wake up." Ellen said as she tried to shake me awake. I jumped realizing that I was sweating and hyperventilating.

" What on earth were you dreaming about?"

" You wouldn't believe me if I told you." I said as she gave me a large mug of tea.

I sipped the tea slowly and turned on the TV. The bus bombing was still headline news. The rolling banner at the bottom of the screen presented all the latest updates. Miraculous survival of the driver. Two dead on the upper deck. Was the driver giving friends an unauthorized lift home? Where was the bomb and who had deposited it onto the bus? So many questions and very few answers. I wondered how much of the information that was being given to the news channels was either truthful or accurate. The warning texts from Stella showed that there was something unusual going on. Nemo and co were going to some effort to distance themselves from any scandal.

I did remember once when I was working as a teacher, a colleague had died in suspicious circumstances. Being afraid of a scandal, the Headmaster warned all the staff to avoid talking to the media about it but that was understandable as the suspect was widely gossiped about and all concerned wanted to make sure that there was a fair trial and justice was done. That was the only remotely similar situation I had ever been in and even then, it had been totally different.

I continued to watch and then the banner on the screen turned red and flashed as it did when a new piece of breaking news happened.

" Photos of the two victims of the number 75 bus bombings have been released by the City Police." The newsreader said gravely.

Two photos appeared on the screen. Both young men in their mid to late twenties. Both looked similar in appearance. Slim faced and smiling. I looked intently at them. I was trying to rack my brains to see if I recognized either of them. One of them did not look familiar at all but I couldn't shake the feeling that I had seen the other man before.

I closed my eyes and then sharply open them again. With his hair slicked back and unsmiling the second man was the man who had sat next to me on the bus and put the note in my pocket. I swallowed a couple of times and nearly choked on my tea.

"Woah. Steady. Blimey there's no rush." Said Ellen.

I didn't reply and just stayed glued to the screen.

"It seems the dead men were work colleagues. They were working for a large financial company in the city centre." The Newsreader continued. "No one seems to be aware of the reasons for both men to have been riding on the out of service bus. The location of the bomb is also unknown but appears to have been a pocket device of some kind as the damage, though extensive appears to have to have been fairly localized, the bottom deck appears to have been relatively unscathed. The driver was completely unharmed but has obviously been traumatized by the experience and is being cared for at an undisclosed location."

The sound of the Newsreader's voice faded away into the background. My dream had proved to be prophetic and I couldn't get over it. Why did he pick me to give his note to and how could I have helped him anyway? I wondered if I'd kept his original note. I got up and went into the bedroom. I went through my jewellery box and found the serviette from last night. Sure, enough underneath the mess of earrings and necklaces, I found it. I stuffed them both into the furthest reaches of the jewellery box and piled as many necklaces, bracelets and earrings on top as possible. I needed to keep everything as safe as possible.

"What are you doing?" Ellen asked. "Are you OK? What's going on? You're being a bit weird."

She sat down on the bed and rubbed my arm.

"I think being mugged has just shaken me up a bit that's all." I half lied.

"Oh, bloody hell of course. You've hardly had any time to rest, you were so busy looking after me. You're the best friend in the world." She said.

I smiled sheepishly and felt bad that I hadn't told Ellen the truth. She was right, we were best friends but the truth was so incredible and I felt that telling her too much might put her in danger and I wouldn't have done that for all the world.

"Anyway, you haven't had a look in that envelope yet." She said.

"It might be something personal. I'm not sure we should." I said.

"Oh, come on. If it's bank statements or invoices we can just put it straight in the bin. It might be a vibrator catalogue or a newsletter for stamp collecting. It could be anything and she obviously wasn't that bothered or she would've come back to pick it up." Ellen said.

She dug me in the ribs and winked at me.

"You know you want to." She said.

"I'm not going to have any peace, otherwise am I?" I said in mock annoyance.

I left the bedroom and picked up the envelope from the kitchen table where I'd left it earlier that morning. Ellen was bouncing around, clearly excited about what we might find in the mystery envelope. I felt more apprehensive, but then I knew things that Ellen obviously didn't. My hands shook slightly as I ripped the envelope open. Inside was a solitary piece of paper. It was slightly glossy and featured a red symbol on a black background. It was slightly reminiscent of a symbol from a propaganda poster. It was eye catching and very stylized. Around the top of the symbol in an arc read the words;

"The Urban Recyclers."

Then underneath in smaller letters it read:

"If you want to help your environment and your community and can spare a few hours call 999 911. We need you."

I noticed that both the word " help" and the last sentence were underlined in red.

"It sounds like a WW1 poster crossed with the A - Team." Ellen said " What the hell's that all about? It's not even a wig catalogue. "

" No Ellen, it's definitely not a wig catalogue." I replied " Unless you want to recycle your wigs."

Ellen pulled a face and went to sit in the lounge while I got dressed. I was surprised that I hadn't heard more about The Urban Recyclers before. Ours was quite a green area and often initiatives were on the local news or posters appeared, often illegally stuck to lampposts. But nothing and though the flyer was maybe a bit over the top, it was eye catching and would surely attract the attention of likeminded people.

"Do you fancy a pizza, my treat?" Ellen called.

"I'm going to be the size of a barn end if we carry on having so many takeaways." I said.

"You could have a small veggie one and I noticed you didn't say no."

"Oh, go on then. " I said slightly pleased truthfully, as I couldn't be bothered to cook.

I set the alarm ready for tomorrow's early start and pondered what to do with the flyer. It didn't seem so important but then there had been a number of instances in the last few days when seemingly unimportant things had taken on an unexpected significance. I decided it might be a good idea to keep it and squirrel it away somewhere safe.

"Are you coming. I'm about to order. I'm bloody starving." Ellen shouted.

"I'm coming, I'm coming." I replied.

I stuffed the flyer under the mattress and went into the lounge.

The TV was still talking away in the background as we made our choices and phoned in the delivery.

"This just in. The partner of Cale Reed, one of the men killed in Wednesday's bus bombing has just been speaking to journalists." The newsreader said.

"Oh, poor woman." Ellen said.

I looked up and saw the woman from the hospital.

"Oh, bloody hell." I said.

"What's up?" Ellen asked.

"She's the woman from the hospital." I replied.

"Bloody hell." Ellen said " Come on then turn it up. I want to hear what she's saying."

I wanted to hear too. There was something slightly strange about her as she seemed to betray very little emotion. She certainly wasn't wearing the desolate appearance of deep grief. As I looked more closely, I realized that she was holding up two pictures. One of her partner, who I now knew was called Cale Reed. The other was the same flyer as she'd dropped in the hospital.

"I have known Cale since we studied together at university. We both studied History and Mass communication. He went to work for a financial company and I worked as a researcher for an environmental charity. We both wanted to help make the world a better place in our own way. Cale was not a terrorist. He was not responsible for the bomb on that bus. He would not have put himself or others in harm's way like that. He was in the wrong place at the wrong time. I want to say to anyone who wants to help remember Cale to donate to our charity, The Urban Recyclers. Whether it's your money or your time both are precious. We need your help. Thank you." She said.

The woman did not stay to answer questions so the journalists were left shouting any they had to the air.

"Brave woman." Ellen said. " I don't think, I could have done that."

"No, me neither." I said.

" I wonder what she meant by him not being a terrorist." She said.

" I dunno. I suppose they don't know who was responsible for detonating the bomb yet. It was either Cale or the other bloke, I suppose." I replied.

The doorbell went and Ellen went downstairs to get the pizzas. I continued to watch the screen, both saddened and intrigued by what I'd just heard.

Along the bottom of the screen, the ticker tape ran with other stories. The latest unemployment figures, the death of someone I'd never heard of and the arrest of someone from The Underground Resistance. I did remember the name but only vaguely.

I realized that I'd forgotten to turn my phone on. As, I did two more messages from Stella popped up.

"Disregard what Cale Reed's widow said. She's not to be trusted." Read the first.

"She didn't give you a flyer, did she?" Read the second.

I dropped my phone on the floor. Ellen reappeared carrying the pizzas.

"Are you ok? " She said.

"Yes, just being a bit clumsy." I replied.

"Weird guy delivering the pizza. " She said. "

"In what way? " I asked.

"He was stood staring at me for ages and then he asked me if I was ok." She said.

"He maybe just fancied you." I teased.

"No, it wasn't that. He asked if I was better. He spoke to me like he knew me. " Ellen replied.

"Maybe he did? " I said

"I don't remember seeing him before in my life. It creeped me out." Ellen replied.

"I'm not surprised. Did he say anything else? "

"He just said tell your friend to get in 10 minutes earlier, Stella will be waiting."

If I ever doubted it before, now I was certain we were being watched.

****

CHAPTER 6

Day 4

Surveillance makes you paranoid. Then again that's part of the point of it. Bentham's Panopticon Principle worked on the idea that prisoners would regulate themselves if they knew they were being watched. So, what happens if you don't know or at least you aren't sure? Ubiquitous cameras get forgotten about, become part of the scenery continuously recording but not preventing. The eye in the sky may see you but it won't necessarily save you.

I couldn't sleep. I was fairly sure by now that Cale Reed was being watched and because he'd approached me, now I and also Ellen, by the sounds of it, were too. Considering the bomb on the bus, it was obvious that he was mixed up in something. But then why approach me and was he being followed by someone else who then killed him. Or was he the killer? But then why bomb an empty bus? None of it made sense. I was beginning to feel we were both in danger and that it had only started when I started working for Nemo and Co.

I was coming to the conclusion that I wanted to leave. No well-paid cleaning job was worth this sort of grief. And yet a large part of me was really fascinated by what was happening. What part did Cale Reed's partner play in all of this and why was Stella warning me off?

I looked at the clock and groaned. Midnight. At least this was the last day I was working this week. I hoped.

****

When I woke up at half past two, I felt I hadn't slept at all. The grog of the last few days felt like it had taken up residence in my joints. I was glad of a further slight snooze on the night bus and incredibly I did manage to wake up at the right stop.

As usual, when I reached the door to the office, it opened before I could even press the buzzer.

"Go straight down to the bottom of the hall, then please turn right instead of left."

I recognized the menace in Stella's voice immediately. It was as polite as ever but even considering her digital tones, it was colder than usual.

I walked down to the bottom of the corridor and turned right. It was a bit of a surprise as I hadn't even realized there was a right turn to be had, as the door was camouflaged by the position of the spotlight. As I reached the door, it opened and I walked into the room. The room itself was dark apart from a dim fluorescent light in the ceiling. It appeared to have a reddish tinge and walls appeared to be upholstered.

It was sparsely furnished with a chair covered in the same material as the walls and a large oak desk in the centre.

"Thank you for coming in slightly earlier. You will be paid of course. I just thought that you and I should have a little chat about how things are going."

The tone of her voice didn't waver. I couldn't see her anywhere in the room but then not every part was visible.

"Sit down on the chair, please. Did you want anything to drink?" She said.

"No thank you." I said. I didn't really trust anything that I'd be given here.

"Suit yourself." She said.

I was beginning to find it difficult to move but didn't want to say anything.

"Did you get my texts and messages?" She asked.

"Yes." I answered. I was feeling as though my wrists and ankles were being clamped to the chair.

"It really is very important that you don't discuss anything that happens here with your friend, Ellen? Is it?" She said.

"Yes."

"Do you know what we do here?"

"Not really."

"We deal in the business of secrets. Secrets and information. It is both very valuable and very important."

I shifted around in my seat.

"These are secrets that can bring down governments or financial institutions."

"Why are you telling me all of this?" I asked. "I only clean the office."

"Because our system is only as strong as our weakest link which is currently you."

I wasn't sure whether to be flattered to be considered as important enough to potentially wreck their system or insulted as the weakest link.

"You must realize we're keeping quite a close eye on you by now. It's not personal, we do it to everyone. We need to know we can trust you. And we can, can't we?"

I didn't say anything, I just nodded.

"You had to go to the hospital with Ellen, yesterday didn't you?" Stella said.

"Yes, we thought she'd been spiked and attacked and wanted to check that she was ok."

"She really needs to be more careful. Anything can happen when you drink. That seemingly harmless man can do untold damage."

Seemed a bit like Stella was blaming Ellen for someone else's bad behaviour but more than that, it felt a bit like a veiled warning.

"But much as I have Ellen's welfare at heart, I'm more concerned with you as my employee. I'm rather anxious at Cale Reed's widow trying to contact you as I implied in my messages to you. She tried to give you a flyer inviting you to a meeting of "The Urban Recyclers", did she not?"

As Stella already knew the answer, I thought it was pointless trying to deny it.

" Yes, I found it a bit weird. I don't know why she picked me. I've never met her before in my life."

"You're new. So, you can be influenced. She doesn't like the sort of things we do here." Stella said.

"But how would she even know who I was? " I asked.

"She watches. Just like we do. But there is one major difference in what we do. We do what we do to protect people. She is merely dangerous and wants to disrupt." Stella replied.

I realized that Stella wanted me to give The Urban Recyclers, a wide berth but with every sentence I just felt more and more intrigued.

"You said that one of the men who was killed used to work here. Why tell me that? I don't understand. If you'd not told me anything, I never would've guessed."

"I think you underestimate how much, The Urban Recyclers want to recruit anyone who works here. Especially anyone new. I wanted to make sure that you know both that there are dangerous people who are watching you, and so are we, to make sure you don't pass on any of our secrets." Stella said.

But who is the more dangerous? I thought.

I wondered how far the surveillance went. Nemo and co seemed to know what was happening within the flat but also when I was outside. I still wasn't sure if I'd been mugged by an actual mugger, one of Stella's spies or an Urban Recycler. Ellen's spiking seemed suspicious now too. But then again was it just that someone had followed us from my flat to the hospital? It seemed an awful lot of effort to ensure someone's loyalty. What sort of secrets were Nemo and Co. keeping?

****

CHAPTER 7

By 12 O'clock, I was home. Ellen had gone. She had an interview and so had to be up and out by 7.45. I was glad of some peace. Though she was my best friend, the last few days had been exhausting. I hadn't expected to have been drawn in to such a web of intrigue. Who would? I couldn't help feeling that anyone who has to resort to the methods that Nemo and co were had something quite significant to hide. I didn't like it. It made me wonder what Cale Reed had to do with it all. Was he a killer or had he been killed? And if so why? Was he a defender or an exposer of those secrets? I had to find out. But in doing so I had to be extremely careful. No more writing lists. Any lists now had to remain in my head because Stella couldn't see in there or at least, I didn't think she could.

****

Cale Reed was sat at the end of my bed. He was looking at me and not saying anything. His face was terribly injured and had a bluish tint. I tried to move but couldn't as he made his way towards me. He reached towards me and I could see the exposed bones in his arm and that two of his fingers were missing. I didn't want to look at him but I couldn't look away. He was appalling to look at but he was also tragic.

"What are you trying to tell me, Cale? " I asked.

He groaned trying to form words that I couldn't fathom. I could also see a lone tear trickling down the side of his face.

He continued groaning with the effort of trying to communicate.

I could make out an o sound to begin with.

"O ... O " He groaned, his voice rising.

I put my hand over his hand and tried to encourage him further.

"D....o....." He said. " D...o...n..."

"Don't? Is that what you're saying?" I asked.

He nodded vigorously.

"T...t....r...r ." He said.

"Treat? Trick?" I asked

He shook his head quickly and firmly.

"T...r...u...u..."

"Trust? Don't trust?" I said.

He nodded again.

" S...s..t...."

Before he could finish, he disappeared into the door way like he'd been pulled backwards into a vacuum. As he vanished, a blinding white light appeared through the bedroom window. It was like a nuclear flash. As it dissipated a figure appeared at the end of the bed.

"Stella." I said.

"You must always be ready." She said " I'm always watching. I have eyes everywhere. But you know that. You're trying to work out how to avoid being seen. But how can you if you don't know where my spies are? Or in fact who my spies are. Just remember what happened to Mr. Reed. He was one of my right-hand men. I thought I could trust him with anything but he developed a conscience. Tiresome really. He could have just left if he didn't like what he was having to do. I would've forgiven him as long as he kept his mouth shut. He'd earned enough money to retire and he could've disappeared. But no, he had to do something. So, then I had to do something too."

Stella paced backwards and forwards at the end of the bed. I was frightened by what she was implying.

"I don't know what you're saying." I said.

"Oh, I think you do. As I said to you, we are the keepers of secrets and we will do anything to make sure that they stay secret. We don't believe in freedom of information. That's a modern concept. We believe in needing to know and most people don't need to know. In fact, most people don't even want to know. Far too busy getting on with the normal everyday stuff of life. But sometimes something happens that ends up threatening this sleepwalking through life. Sometimes that doesn't matter when no one of any importance or no secrets are threatened. But sometimes, the opposite happens. The very pillars of this society could fall and then what happens? Disintegration and the stuff of anarchy. Any semblance of a constructive, working society falls into ruin. We cannot allow that to happen and we will use any means, reasonable or not to uphold things. To maintain things as they are. Because things work as they are."

"Do they?" I thought " And for who?"

Stella kept on talking. I realized that she found a sadistic enjoyment in trying to intimidate me and I found myself comparing her perfect, but cold, chrome face to Cale Reed's broken one. I had no doubt that Stella thought herself to be a patriot and Cale a traitor. I was beginning to think it was more like the other way around. What secrets were worth murdering a man for and changing his life story? I looked up and saw that Stella had gone and all that was left in her place was what looked like an old Coke can. At least that's what I thought it was. I couldn't really tell. It looked like it had been blown apart.

****

Day 5

I came to gradually to the sound of the TV talking away in the background. The sentences came and went in nonsensical groups as they do when you're half asleep and only certain words drift into your consciousness. " Explosion" " Soft drink probably Coke", " Hat on a lamppost " " lizard called Boris." I wondered if the TV was actually in my dream and I was actually still asleep. It was no more surreal than the dreams I seemed to be having lately.

I checked my phone. Two messages, both from Ellen. There was thankfully, for once, no messages from Stella.

"Got the job!!! Yesss! "

I smiled. Ellen had been wanting to get a solicitor's job for years since we both graduated but opportunities were few and far between.

"Now working for Nemo and co. Really well paid and have to sign Official Secrets Act and NDA. I could tell you, but I'll have to kill you. ;) See you later. Drinks on me."

I couldn't believe it. She'd been headhunted like me. No interview for years and then this. Too good to be true as it was for me. It could be a coincidence but I didn't think so. The same morning as Stella gave me her veiled warning and then Ellen suddenly gets a last-minute interview. She was being watched like me, likely because of me. I needed to warn her against it but didn't know how. I didn't want to make things worse and put her in worse danger than she was in already. I decided to ring her anyway. If she could make her excuses, maybe she wouldn't get mixed up in all of this. I doubted it but I had to try.

I dialled Ellen's number. It didn't even ring.

"The number you have dialled has not been recognized please hang up."

I tried again.

"The number you have dialled has not been recognized please hang up."

I checked the number again. It was definitely hers. It had been disconnected. A wave of fear swept over me. Where was Ellen now and was she in danger? I had no possible way of knowing.

As I was weighing up what to do, another message from an anonymous number pinged into my inbox.

Not now, Stella, I thought. But when I opened it. It wasn't from Stella.

"Reed asked for your help and now you need ours. We will send a taxi round for you. You will be blindfolded in case you're caught. Wear a hat and sunglasses and get into the right-hand rear door. Do exactly as you are told once you get into the taxi. We still need your help. This is non-negotiable."

It was signed "The UR". Stella was right, we were being watched by The Underground Resistance. Was she right about why? It was risky meeting them, no doubt but Ellen's safety may well depend on it. I didn't feel there was much option.

****

CHAPTER 8

Within five minutes, the doorbell rang.

"Taxi."

I recognized the voice. I quickly put a hat on, put my keys in my pocket and walked out of the door. I opened the right-hand door as I was asked and sat on the back seat. A young woman tied a blindfold around my eyes and checked my bag.

"You've no recording devices, have you? Can you give your phone please? I will give you it back but we need to ensure that we aren't followed." She said.

I reluctantly handed my phone over thinking that if the Underground Resistance intended to kidnap me now, there wasn't an awful lot that I could do about it. And if I was no one was likely to report it. I would become one of the many missing people who never reappear. The woman turned the phone off. I felt the taxi travelling over speed bumps and driving around corners. The gentle swaying movement made my drowsy and I found myself drifting off to sleep.

"Come on sleepy head, we're here. " The woman said.

I woke with a start.

"How long have we been here?" I asked.

"Doesn't matter." The woman said " I'll help you inside. We need you to keep your blindfold on until we know we can trust you. Give me your arm." She said, not unkindly.

She opened the door nearest her and I felt a blast of cold air blow into my face. She took my arm and pulled me gently out of the car door.

"See you later, babe. " The Taxi Driver called out.

I knew I'd recognized the voice. It looked like his governor had been a different person than I thought it was. I felt very vulnerable being guided. Intermittently, I tripped up over uneven ground. The wind continued to blow and whipped around my face and ears. It seemed we'd been walking outside for hours but soon enough we were walking in a narrow stone corridor as the temperature dropped further and our footsteps echoed every time that they hit the floor.

"We're nearly there now. " The woman said "It gets quite low here so watch your head."

She gently grabbed the top of my head and pushed it downwards.

"Keep it down until I tell you." she said

I felt like this was in itself a test to see how I would cope. It reminded me of an assault course I had completed as a youngster. We were tied to two other people and had to crawl through a stone pipe. One of the girls I was tied to, panicked mid tunnel and pulled backwards, the other girl kept moving forward and I was stuck in the tunnel being pulled in opposite directions by the two of them. I wondered if I was going to be pulled in half. It felt quite a lot like this whole situation. Being in the dark and pulled between two camps unsure if either had my best interests at heart.

The woman guided me towards a chair and helped me to sit down. She then removed the blindfold and I had to blink a couple of times to get used to the light. I looked around and realized that I was sat in an abandoned bunker. The concrete arches above made it feel slightly like a ruined church. I could see a table a few metres in front of me with an angle poise lamp in the furthest left-hand corner. To the left and slightly in front of the table was a woman. It wasn't possible to see all of her face, but even at the distance I was sat away from her, I could see she was Cale Reed's widow.

There were two other figures slightly behind her at either side. They were entirely in shadow and I couldn't see if they were men or women, or if they were armed.

"I'm glad you came. Thank you for cooperating. Nemo and Co. will be bugging your phone so we'll give you a burner phone that they can't track it. That's if you want to help us. We hope so. We need you to do a trade with us so we can help you get Ellen back." She said.

It was obvious that they weren't offering to help with Ellen from any pure sense of altruism. I wasn't sure if they were any better than Nemo and Co. at all. But they hadn't taken my friend and through Cale Reed, they'd already asked for my help once and I didn't want what had happened to him to happen to any-body else.

"Ok. But can I ask you a few things because there's so much I don't understand. " I asked.

"Ask away." The woman said. " I can't promise I'll answer you but I'll do my best."

"Firstly, what is your name? I don't feel right not being able to call you anything." I said.

"You can call me Nico Tucker." She said.

"It's not your real name is it? " I said

"No" She said. " No more than Cale Reed was my partner's name but that doesn't really matter does it?"

"I suppose not." I said.

"So, what's next or is that it?" Nico asked.

"I suppose what I really want to know is what kind of secrets do Nemo and Co. deal in that they feel it's justified to spy on me and Ellen, murder Cale and then kidnap Ellen? I'm only a cleaner, what threat can I be to them?" I asked

Nico exhaled very slowly and stayed silent for a minute. I wasn't entirely sure that she would answer my question at all.

"I never really worked there for long myself but as you know, Cale did for a few years. Stella has obviously given you the spiel about needing to keep the secrets or society will break down." Nico replied.

I nodded.

"Nemo and Co. has secret information relating to high crimes and misdemeanors concerning Presidents and governments throughout the world. They are kept securely in their system of data vaults but that's not all. Extremely wealthy people also pay for the same service. But it isn't only about the storage of information. It's also about the changing of information. Sometimes to something more palatable sometimes to something more destructive?" Nico said.

"What do you mean?" I asked.

"For example, if there is say a political figure who has some kind of sexual deviancy and a reporter who has discovered it and is ready to print the story, Nemo and Co. will get involved. They will take any information from the computers owned by the journalist through hacking and alter it so any evidence becomes null and void. But they will also simultaneously disseminate information that means that the journalist themselves will be smeared. They have a number of print and TV journalists, internet trolls and bots in their pocket. Some are true believers and others are simply ruining other people to protect themselves from the same thing happening to them. Their skill is that they can make it look extremely realistic and so public opinion is swayed and then at least while the political figure is in office, it is far more difficult than usual to hold them accountable.

After they leave office it may be a whole different story dependent on what their interests are. They could be brought down. They could become a member of the board. It all depends."

I couldn't stop myself from pulling a face as Nico was telling me all of this.

"You don't believe me?" She said.

"Well, it does sound a bit like the lizard people ruling the earth? "I said.

"Yes, I understand your scepticism but ask yourself why did they kill Cale? Why did they headhunt and kidnap Ellen and why are they watching you?" She said.

"But I've only got your word for it and you were obviously watching us too. Hence The Taxi Driver." I said.

"Yes, we were. But that Taxi Driver came in pretty useful when you were mugged didn't, he?" Nico said.

"So, the mugging wasn't down to you?" I asked.

"No that was one of Stella's thugs. The internet cafe you went to is run by one of hers and they phoned up to let them know. The only reason you haven't had your contract terminated was because you were clever enough to put the serviette in your shoe in the toilet and they didn't see." Nico replied.

I sat on the chair shaking my head. It was all too unbelievable. I felt as if I had walked into some dystopian spy novel. But I hadn't. It was all real.

"How does Stella fit into all this? What is she?" I asked.

"That's a very good question." Nico replied. " Have you actually seen her? Well, she's not really a her, being an automaton."

"She's a robot? Are you serious? I have only spoken to her or had messages from her. We've been in the same room but she's been in the dark." I replied.

"Stella is the great enforcer. She's the ultimate psychopath but without the superficial charm. She's there to manipulate and intimidate. To make sure that all Nemo and Co. employees do as they're told. She's not always vicious but she expects absolute loyalty and if she finds any evidence to the contrary, she will do what she can to terminate people's contracts and sometimes people's lives."

"Like Cale you mean." I said.

"Yes." She nodded " He wasn't the first and he won't be the last until we bring down Nemo and Co. And deactivate Stella."

I sat in my chair quietly for a moment trying to take everything in.

"How do you know so much about Stella, Nico? " I asked

"I know as much as I do because I helped create her. " She said.

****

CHAPTER 9

My head was spinning. I couldn't take it all in.

"So, you helped create the robot who killed your partner?" I asked. "Why would you want to create anything who helped to kill anyone?"

"It wasn't my intention for that to happen. I didn't want that robot technology to be used to destroy anything. It was a utopian ideal to start with." Nico replied.

"How?" I said.

"What do you know about robot technology?" Nico asked.

"Not much." I replied.

"I worked on Stella's inception about 15 years ago. Long before she was ever turned into the weapon she eventually became. The brief then was to make her into a helpful sidekick if you like just to aid any company and help to make them more efficient but in a way that helped to aid the human employees to have slightly more leisure time and follow other activities. That of course didn't happen because greed and power got in the way, as it invariably does.

About five years ago, the university I was working for was approached by Nemo and Co. who offered them staggering amounts of money to buy both the technology and staff, who were willing to move and work for them. They showed up with what seemed a relatively benign proposal concerning turning our prototype into an automaton that would help intelligence services collect and manipulate intelligence on targets, the idea being that as an automaton, they'd be less open to manipulation and becoming a double agent themselves.

The whole idea bothered me right from the start as we'd seen incidences of employees in other firms being targeted in ways that we hadn't intended. Maybe because of political beliefs of themselves or someone they were close to. People were being identified as vulnerabilities to the system and sacked."

"So, you stopped working on the project? You didn't move over to work for Nemo and Co. for any length of time?" I said.

"No, I didn't. I've always been wary of grey figures waving around lots of money. It usually doesn't end well. If you add in secrecy on top of that, then that goes double. So, I left, deciding not to be any part of it and hoping that nothing too nefarious would happen next but unfortunately, I was naive. I became involved with "The Urban Recyclers" about a year after I stopped working for the university.

At that time, they were an environmental group who basically did what the name suggests, setting up projects that helped to enable urban places to become more sustainable. There was some direct action involved in that too. Sometimes we squatted in commercial property that had remained dormant for years and did them up or decorated abandoned railway carriages that had been left to rust and made them into cafes or libraries.

We managed to do it without too much interference at first, because sorting out the carriages helped to make them less of an eyesore and it also meant that it saved money for the rail companies who would have had to have paid companies to come in and dismantle them and saved money for the councils maintaining library buildings as we supplied the books and furniture ourselves from things we no longer needed. It was once we started to squat in the abandoned commercial properties that the trouble started.

We had always chosen our places with the explicit aim to make each abandoned building useful, clean and better than we found it. So, we took our salvage experts and building experts in, contacted the owner to ask if they had any plans for the buildings because if they did, we would disappear and leave them to it. The great majority of owners just ignored our queries and so when that happened, we took ownership, saved any property inside the building and stored it in order to send it on to them and do the building up."

"Isn't that theft though? " I asked.

Nico laughed and rubbed her hands.

"You could call it that certainly." She said. " We like to call it guerilla redistribution. We give them plenty of opportunities to do something useful with it themselves. We keep things safe for them and return them and we ultimately make things better with no cost to anyone but our selves. The sad truth is that some of these property owners have so many properties that they don't miss one. Or that they merely want to own things for owning things sake, even if those things are derelict and could be used to help other people. Which is worse? "

I shifted slightly in my chair.

"So, you said that once you started taking over these buildings then the trouble started. What do you mean? " I asked.

"It was quite subtle at first. We began to notice negative posts about us on social media. Nothing extraordinary just the usual troll abuse but the level of posts ramped up significantly and quickly.

Then the local newspapers started to run negative stories. We'd gone from being the eccentric do gooders who didn't end up causing too much trouble, to being Eco-terrorists who were threatening the very existence of the local area. So far so relatively normal. But then a couple of our activists went missing. People often lead quite free-spirited lives in our community so to begin with, we didn't really notice what was happening. But then a few relatives started getting in touch because the disappearances were out of character. These people were vanishing without a trace and then a few months later bodies were turning up and they'd died under weird circumstances. "Nico said

"Like how?" I asked.

"There was a young woman. We'll call her Jane. She was found under a bridge with a syringe sticking out of her arm. So what you might say? Plenty of people develop addictions quite suddenly? But Jane was so clean living, she didn't drink or smoke and she wasn't even interested in hallucinogenics. It was very much out of character and she had a very good relationship with her family. Do you remember our Taxi Driver?" Nico asked.

I nodded.

"He was Jane's dad and he vowed to do everything in his power to bring Nemo and Co. down because of what they did to his daughter." Nico said.

"But why did they choose her? " I asked.

"Because she was an idealist but also because of the sort of person she was. They knew that someone as pure of heart as her, who we knew would never overdose like that, in those circumstances would strike a real blow to the organization. We would know that she'd been murdered but they could smear her through their various channels and we could do very little about it. No one would believe us and because of the way that such deaths are investigated. It's rare that investigators would look into too deeply. Some would, but it's rare. It was a kind of psychological warfare. " Nico replied.

"What did Jane do? " I asked.

"She helped source stuff for the libraries. She often went knocking on doors looking for books that people didn't want or need anymore. She also became our first undercover agent in Nemo and Co. She happened to already work there and just helped us out on the weekend. One day when she was working, she caught sight of some documents that another employee had kept open on their laptop. She was so appalled by what she saw that she suggested that she went undercover and found out what she could and then passed it all onto us the idea being that we could then use it when the time was right. She managed to work there for about a month before she was caught and then they got rid of her and the other employee who she'd managed to spy on."

"My God..." I said.

"Yes, he was found hanging from a light fitting in the room of a brothel in his pants. You might have seen the story in the paper? All of this is Stella's work. It is what she is there for. To eliminate threats with no conscience. Even the most indoctrinated humans are capable of having second thoughts. There are of course psychopaths, but most of us are not machines." Nico said.

"Then there was Cale. " I said.

"Yes. Stella ordering the assassination of Cale is intended to destroy me personally and the organization as a whole. She assesses that by painting us as a terrorist group and smearing us in the media, that we will be made and illegal group and that gives more opportunities for members to be incarcerated on little evidence. Thus, disrupting the work of the underground and letting Nemo and Co carry on with their work unopposed." Nico said.

I took a very long deep breath.

"What I don't understand is why they haven't picked you up or infiltrated here. Even why, and I apologize for saying this, they haven't assassinated you too?"

"There's a very important reason why we live and work in this bunker. Cold War architecture. It's quite useful for keeping out satellite trackers and mobile signals don't work down here. Our communications are paper or burner phones. No contracts. Speaking of burner phones as I said earlier, if you do decide to join us, we will give you one and don't worry about topping it up we can do that remotely. So, think hard if you definitely want to join us. It will definitely help Ellen. We don't expect her to help us but we do expect you to keep us secret. "

"That may be difficult. Ellen being how she is." I said.

"I'm sure it will be, but both of your safety depends on it." Nico said.

"Is that a veiled threat?" I asked

"Do you think Nemo and Co. will just let you both carry on living your lives as they are if they find out that you're working for us? They're watching you already and they have kidnapped Ellen. However dangerous you may think that we are, we haven't killed anyone and we don't intend to. We do want to de-activate Stella though and if possible, make redundant the technology that created her. So, do you need any time to think? It's up to you, but the longer you take, the harder it'll be for Ellen. You've got a 24-hr. window as we've set up some diversionary tactics to keep Stella busy. We can't guarantee any longer than that." Nico said.

"I only have one question really because as things stand, I don't think there's any choice." I said.

"Ok, fire away." Nico said.

"I'm curious what does the name Stella stand for? It's obviously an acronym." I said.

"Yes, it is. Stella stands for Surveillance and Truth Eliciting Lethal Automaton. Basically, exactly what she is." Nico said.

"Who came up with that? It wasn't you was it? " I asked.

I didn't know whether to be impressed or disgusted. The fact that Stella's whole reason for being was to be a manipulative murdering spy with no conscience was even more profoundly disturbing now that it was confirmed in her very name.

"Oh lord no." Nico said. " I would've used more numbers. It's a very showy name. Extremely narcissistic but then if you get to meet the brains behind Nemo and Co., you'll realize that they are an order of magnitude worse than Stella is. She has been programmed that way. What she does is terrible but the people who saw the need for her and made her the way she is are worse.

They are ideologues who are so wedded to those ideas that they have created a being who will kill for them to maintain the dominance of that idea."

"Am I ever likely to meet these people though? Being the lowest of the low in that place? They're not likely to introduce me to their CEO anytime soon, are they?" I said.

Nico looked me right in the eye.

"You think yourself to be invisible. There are advantages to that sometimes you know. Stella is keeping quite a close eye on you at the moment but that won't last forever. They only do it at the level that they're doing it with you when you're new. After about 2 months, they give up. They are like every other operation; they have to watch the pennies. You just have to keep your nose clean for a few more weeks until Stella gets bored and then she'll find some other rookie to follow. Have you noticed a man, in specs, with a gold tooth following you about?"

I tried to think. That did sound vaguely familiar.

·"Possibly in the pub and I think he might've delivered a couple of takeaways too. I think Ellen met him and thought he was a bit weird." I said.

"She's right." said Nico. "His name's Lawson and he's a subtle as a brick, but he's also one of Stella's favourites. He can be really quite nasty but he's also quite easy to give the slip if you know his method. We can help you with that. Anyway, we need to get Ellen back so I'm going to call for your taxi. So, here's your burner phone. It's just a basic model no internet, etc. Makes it harder to trace. Keep it on, unless we tell you to turn it off. We'll contact you on it and send you instructions. "

"Where is Ellen?" I asked

"I'm not going to tell you that but don't worry. She'll be back by tonight. She'll have been drugged again so be prepared to keep quite a close eye on her but we'll have given her an antidote so she should be fine. I will check in with you later to make sure and we can always help if necessary." Nico said.

"Thank you." I said as a figure came behind me and put a blindfold on me once more.

"No thank you." Said Nico.

I suddenly had the feeling for the second time in as many weeks that I selling off a part of myself and was very frightened of the consequences.

****

CHAPTER 10

The taxi ride home was very quiet. I was pretty shell shocked after what I'd heard. I just wanted to zone out as much as I could. I had very mixed feelings about helping The Underground Resistance but they definitely seemed like the lesser of the evils. Speaking to Nico Tucker had fed my paranoia further. I was hoping that Lawson was a figment of my imagination but he obviously wasn't. I didn't enjoy the feeling of being followed, but at least I knew for sure now that it was going on. Not that it was much comfort really.

Soon enough, the taxi pulled up and kept its engine running on idle signalling that it was time to get out. Someone helped me out of the taxi and took off my blindfold. I could see that it was The Taxi Driver.

"I'm sorry about Jane." I said.

"Thanks love." He said.

I pulled my hat down over my eyes and went back up into the flat.

****

I sat watching the news in bed waiting for Ellen to call or turn up on the doorstep. It was awful to think that she'd been drawn into all of this whole thing when it was nothing to do with her. Especially to the extent where she had been purposely misled, drugged and kidnapped.

I was afraid to see what kind of state she would be in when I saw her next. I also wondered how on earth," The Underground Resistance" knew where she was and how they would rescue her?

I hovered like an edgy parent to be waiting for their child to be born. Then all at once, the bell went. It was The Taxi Driver.

"Alright babe. Can you open the door, I've got a delivery for you."? He said.

I buzzed them both in. Ellen was unconscious but breathing and had been carried up the stairs in a fireman's lift. A small purplish bruise was starting to radiate outwards underneath her left eye. I gasped. The Taxi Driver set her down gently on the settee.

"Real bastards this lot, babe. They've given her a good dose so you'll need a bucket nearby I'm afraid." He said.

As he talked, I noticed the red marks on his knuckles. He looked down and chuckled.

"Oh that. I gave that Lawson a right pasting. Serves the git right. Stella's getting sloppy. Not much either of them could do about it. They're getting too clever for their own good and too bold."

"Can you tell me where she was?" I asked.

"No can do I'm afraid. Nico's orders. Ellen won't remember either so no point asking her. One last message from Nico. If you want to do any more research on Nemo and Co, take the number 7 bus and hop on the underground to Brixton. Go into info city and ask for Denzil. Lawson won't dare show his face down there. The Yardies have got a hit out on him because of something he did down there. Or you can text me, I'll take you if Nico don't have me on a job. My number's in the burner phone." The Taxi Driver answered.

And with a cheery wave, he was gone.

****

CHAPTER 11

Our night started with delirium and copious puking. It was like Ellen was rattling. I dreaded to think what she'd been given. She didn't know where she was and I cried looking at the pitiable figure whose dreams had been made a mockery of in the sadistic game of manipulation that Nemo and Co appeared to be playing. I never hated anyone or anything as much as that organisation at that moment. It was its utter disregard for a person's humanity. It's making of Ellen into another mere cog of its machinery to be abused and disregarded in its quest to maintain itself and its masters.

I didn't like the white-hot anger that burned in my belly. I could see how easy it was to become radicalised for a cause. When the people you love are destroyed. When humans are disregarded and become numbers, things. When you become an irrelevance, a nothing, a shadow? I had to channel it somehow as I kept Ellen's head up. I listened to her crying as a dark reality descended. Her dream job didn't exist, she'd been taken advantage of again for the second time in a matter of days. Deliberately and calculatedly. She wept as she knew something was wrong but didn't know why. She knew she'd been duped, but couldn't remember any of it. It was like the tragedy of dementia. Losing the meaning gradually of anything you ever were.

After 3 O'clock and washing her hair, I felt she was safe enough to leave sleeping on the settee as I dragged myself of to bed.

I felt myself drifting off. Half asleep, I heard a very loud noise but it felt unreal as part of a dream. What seemed like a minute later, I heard the buzzer ring? I considered ignoring it but it became insistent and I didn't want it to wake Ellen.

"Hello?" I said.

"Love it's me. Come quickly." It was The Taxi Driver. I checked on Ellen and she wasn't there. I pulled my jacket on and ran down stairs.

A scene of carnage greeted me as I opened up the front door. A crumpled car whose owner was stood at the side of it, head in his hands. Around the car were a small crowd gawping. Classic rubberneckers, taking notes on a tragedy. I couldn't see what they were looking at first then slowly it began to dawn on me. I saw a couple of feet under the car, one shoe off in the road and still wearing the other one. They were both Ellen's.

****

CHAPTER 12

They say in traumatic incidents everything slows down. It's true and I couldn't make sense of anything. I just stood there. Numb. I couldn't move towards her; I couldn't do anything. I couldn't say anything either when the Police officer moved towards me. I opened my mouth but nothing came out. Before I knew it, The Taxi Driver came up and spoke to the Police officer in hushed tones. He came back to me and guided me by the elbow to his cab. Then he opened the back door and bundled me in.

"Not good babe. Not good at all but I can take you to the hospital and then I want you text me and I'll come and pick you up. You need to be around mates at a time like this ok?" He said.

I could only nod as I was still struck dumb. I didn't know what had happened. Had Ellen run in front of the car? Was she hallucinating or depressed? Or had one of Stella's croneys somehow taken hold of her again and pushed her in front of the car? Considering what Nico Tucker had told me, I couldn't know. Maybe I would never know. But then maybe that was the whole point?

"What do you think happened?" I managed to say in a strangled voice.

"I don't know love but I just came around the corner and saw Ellen injured in the road." The Taxi Driver said.

"Were you coming to pick me up for something?" I asked.

"No. For once I really just happened to be in the area looking for a fare on my way home." He said.

"So, I don't need to be blindfolded then?" I asked

"No. We're off to the hospital to see Ellen, babe, aren't we?" He spoke gently, the way you do to a small child.

I just nodded and drew my knees up to my chest. I was glad of the size of the cab. Anything smaller would've seemed claustrophobic. I watched the early morning city rising again. It had a different feel to usual. It seemed hard and sinister. I could see the mirrored sky scrapers cutting into the sky like lasers. I felt I could see Stella's face in all of them. She wasn't laughing or angry or sad. She was impassive. Unmoved by everything going on around her. We were mired in chaos; us tiny fragile beings and she was a chrome giant looking down on all of us. Expressionless. Just watching and analysing.

****

"I can't stay with you for your good or mine. But just text me from your burner phone ok? Wait for me by the reception and don't talk to anyone until I get to you." The Taxi Driver said.

I just nodded dumbly and wandered into the hospital. It was the loneliest moment of my life.

The glass doors swished open and I found myself back in the accident and emergency reception sitting and looking at the same characters as I had just a few days earlier. This time I looked at all of them and wondered if they were another Lawson, a faceless spy sent by Stella. How would I even know?

I spoke to the receptionist and asked about Ellen. But not being family, I couldn't get much information other than that she had been admitted, and was still alive. I left my two phone numbers and left the building. All I wanted to do was walk. The numbness was beginning to disappear but the pain was seeping in and I wanted to run away from it. So, I walked in no particular direction and just kept going. I must've walked for miles and miles until I came to a cafe in a rundown area that I didn't recognize. I went in and ordered some dry toast and a strong cup of tea.

I went to sit down and tried to drink the tea and eat the toast but I was struggling to swallow. The cafe owner was on the phone and nodded when I looked up and noticed. I could only sit there without moving. I wasn't able to take anything in. The door opened I looked up and noticed The Taxi Driver coming towards me.

"What are you doing here?" I asked "How did you find me? I didn't text you."

"You see Trevor behind the counter. He owns the gaff and he's also my brother. He gave me a ring." The Taxi Driver said.

"How did he know who I was?" I said.

"He's one of ours. He knew about everything that's been going on. He can be trusted. You haven't sussed it out yet babe, have you?" He said.

I shook my head not knowing what he meant.

"I'm your bodyguard. Nico asked me to keep an eye on you. So, I'm afraid I'll be around like a bad smell. We've got to keep you safe. So, drink up and I'll take you for a drive." He said.

****

CHAPTER 13

Day 6

The early morning sights filtered through the cab window. The low sunlight highlighted the delivery men and barrow boys. They reminded me of a Renaissance painting. The Taxi Driver drove in silence. He was sensitive enough to realize that I couldn't talk. I could only watch the world go by in silence. I realized Nico had been very wise in choosing The Taxi Driver to keep an eye on me. He was like a bear and unlike Lawson, I couldn't help but feel that he had both mine and Ellen's best interests at heart. I don't know how long we drove for. Time had really lost any meaning. We drove through markets and docks, through tower blocks and the financial district watching the stock brokers and traders fizzing around the streets like bees.

We drove past the parliament and noticed a number of high-profile figures on their phones or huddling in dark corners scheming. I noticed the homeless people sitting in the door-ways. Some were huddled in dirty blankets with cardboard signs, alone. Others were talking and laughing, begging to look after their dogs while they themselves starved. I marvelled at how close the politicians were to some of their constituents and they didn't even notice they were there.

We carried on to the edge of the river and the taxi driver pulled up at a burger van.

"What do you want to eat? " He asked.

"Nothing. Not hungry. " I replied.

"I'll get you something little. If you can't manage it, fine. But you need get something down ya neck."

I just shrugged.

He soon returned with a cup full of soup.

"Just sip at it love. I promise it'll help a bit. We need to get going then. I just got a text from my mate who works in the hospital. She can get you in to see Ellen. "

"Do you know every one? I said.

"I have me mates like everyone else." He said.

"Is she in The Underground? " I asked.

"She might be but all you need to know is that she's a friend. Anyway, drink up. We need to smuggle you in." He replied.

****

CHAPTER 14

Trying to avoid being tracked in an age of CCTV is almost impossible but only almost. It helps to know where all the cameras are. The Taxi Driver was an expert at that. There were more twists and turns than a crime novel in the journey we took down to the hospital. We stopped off at a strip of garages and swapped cars and another driver took over The Taxi Driver's cab. We watched as she drove off and saw how after about twenty seconds a small Fiat started following her.

We continued our journey in an old mini. I wondered if Nemo and Co had a backup car there just in case, to follow us. But it appeared not. It seemed they weren't as rigorous as they thought they were.

"Janey'll keep old Lawson busy for a while. Don't you worry about that." Chuckled The Taxi Driver

"Janey?" I asked.

"Yes, my sister. That's who my Jane was named after. She used to be a test driver. She's pretty good at giving them the slip or causing a distraction when necessary." He said.

"Shit. Don't tell me..." I started.

"Don't worry babe. I won't." He said and winked.

I shook my head and smiled slightly. It was the first time since Ellen's incident. I was relieved that she was still alive.

"There's an outfit that you need to put on before we get there. It's in that little bag next to you on the back seat."

"I dread to think." I said.

I looked inside the bag and found some cleaning overalls.

"Bit of a busman's holiday, I'm afraid babe."

I rolled my eyes and looked heavenward.

"I suppose at least I'll have a bit on an idea of what I'm talking about if someone challenges me." I said.

"That's the spirit." The Taxi Driver said and patted me on the shoulder.

"So, we're going to drive around to one of the side entrances. There's one with very little camera range so that's where we're going to go. Netty, who's going to let you in will sort out an identity badge for you and do any explaining initially for you. She'll get you upstairs into the ICU where you'll get the chance to see Ellen. You've only got half an hour and you may not get the chance to actually get into her room. But they are glass from floor to ceiling so you will at least see her. Keep your eyes peeled and you might get the chance to sneak in. Ok. You understand?"

I nodded. He pulled over into a lay-by and I squeezed into the back seat. I quickly got changed and put my other clothes into the plastic bag. I climbed back into the front seat and stuffed the bag into the glove box.

"Right so, I'll drop you off and then I'm going to swap cars again with Janey. Remember you've got half an hour after I drop you off with Netty." I nodded.

We turned into the car park of the hospital and the drove down a maze of side roads and back alleyways. It was 8 o'clock and so many of the staff were turning up ready to change shifts. We reached the side entrance and I noticed a small dark-haired woman in cleaning overalls motioning vigorously. The Taxi Driver dropped me off and pointed at his watch. I moved quickly towards Netty, who handed me a lanyard with a faked ID fastened to it, which included my picture.

"How?" I started to ask.

"We've got ways and means." Netty said. " Now follow my lead and try to avoid talking if you can, ok? "

I nodded dumbly and grabbed the cleaning cart that Netty passed to me and followed on after her.

We soon made it to the double doors of a service lift. Netty pressed a button and we stepped inside. The lift was empty apart from us.

"Right, we need to be quick because people can step in here at any time. I will get you into the ICU. It's the 6th floor and there are plenty of staff on there who will wonder who you are and what you're doing there. Luckily for us one of the cleaning staff have called in sick and so you are now the agency cleaner for half an hour. The actual agency cleaner is on floor 8 at the moment and working their way down so you shouldn't have too many problems. I'll explain to anyone we see, I'm showing you the ropes, you don't know much English, etc."

The lift door opened and two porters stepped in. They had their backs to us but nonetheless Netty held a finger to her lips. They both only stayed in the lift for one floor then got out. As they turned sideways, I thought one reminded me of someone familiar.

"What is it?" Said Netty

"One of those porters looked really familiar but I can't place them." I said

"Does it matter? " She said.

"I suppose not." I said but for some reason my heart sank and I didn't know why.

We reached the Sixth floor and we both got out. Netty motioned for me to follow her down the corridor opposite and to wait at the reception as she spoke to one of the nurses.

She motioned again and walked us both past the reception and the camera that was fixed opposite it.

"She's in the room at the end of this corridor. I'll be leaving you in a second but I've told them that your English is poor so just look puzzled and try not to say anything. If it looks too risky to go into Ellen's room, then don't do it. You can see her through the window. You've got 20 minutes to see her and be downstairs and by the back door for our friend to come and pick you up. So, make sure to check your watch." Netty said and with that she was gone.

I nodded at her and the nurse at the reception and walked with my cleaning cart to the end of the corridor. I could see Ellen through the window. Nothing prepares you for seeing a loved one hooked up to machinery that is keeping them alive. Her poor face was purple and bruised and both of her legs were bolted into cages to keep them straight. I blinked back tears knowing that there was very little I could do here in the time I had.

I walked into the room and set the cleaning cart in the left-hand corner. I checked my watch and saw that I only had 5 minutes before I needed to set off back downstairs again.

"Ellen, I don't know if you can hear me. Or how this happened but I want to tell you that if anyone pushed you in front of that car, I'm going to make sure they face justice for what they've done. I promise you. " I said.

I squeezed her hand and then left the room. I started to make my way towards the service lift. As I made my way down the corridor, I saw the porter again.

"Can you go to room one and clean up there's been a bit of a furore?" He said.

I nodded but didn't say anything and moved quickly, past room one and into the service lift. I looked again at my watch and saw that I had five minutes until The Taxi Driver. I racked my brains trying to remember where I'd seen the porter.

I left the cleaning cart by the back door and just as I opened it, The Taxi Driver drove up.

I got in and sat on the back seat and let out a large sigh. Then it hit me.

"Oh my God." I gasped.

"What's up, babe? " He said.

"It was Lawson. Lawson without the glasses." I said.

"Who was? " He asked.

"There was a porter going up towards Ellen's room, just as I was leaving. " I said " And it was Lawson."

****

CHAPTER 15

The Taxi Driver got out his phone and rang a number. No one replied at first. Then a minute or so later, his phone rang.

"Netty. " He said " Lawson's poking around the ICU. He's making his way towards Ellen. "

He remained silent for a moment then nodded.

"Do what you need to do. We'll disappear. Let me know what happens." He said then put the phone down.

"We'll disappear? " I asked, incredulously. " What about Ellen?"

"If he's got to her already. There's nothing we can do but if hasn't we can't be around for what happens next." He said.

"What do you mean?" I asked. "Or maybe I don't want to know."

"Trust me, babe, you don't." He said with a grim look on his face.

I didn't like what he was implying but I also didn't like that Ellen could be attacked or even murdered while she was in hospital.

"Why couldn't Nico get Ellen a bodyguard?" I asked.

"She has. Netty's her bodyguard." He said.

"Netty?" I said "But she's a cleaner."

"Indeed, she is love. Indeed, she is." He said. "Now put your blindfold on. We're off to see Nico."

****

I was back in the ICU. All of the windows were open and the curtains were blowing violently in the breeze. I could see Ellen in the bed or rather she was floating just above it, tethered just by the equipment that was keeping her alive.

Netty was sweeping up and down the corridor with a blank look on her face. She didn't seem able to see me as every time we passed each other, she just carried on looking straight ahead. I kept on walking trying to get closer to Ellen's room but it was like I was on an airport conveyor belt that was moving too quickly. I was moving to stand still. I tried to reach forward and could see three other figures in the room with Ellen. From this angle, I couldn't quite see who they were.

Suddenly I shot forward as if carried by the wind. Stood around Ellen's bed were a man and a woman. I could only see them in silhouette. They both appeared to be holding remote controls in their hands and intermittently they pressed buttons. I didn't realize it at first but those buttons seemed to be controlling Ellen's bed and her own body. So, every time the man pressed a button, Ellen either rose or fell, dependent on which button he was pressing.

"Stop it, stop it!" I screamed at him but he didn't seem to hear me. If he did, he completely ignored me.

I then looked at the woman and tried to work out who or what her remote control was controlling. Just at that moment, I shot forward again. The awful realization dawned that she was controlling me. I was brought forward again sharply until I could see completely into Ellen's room.

Just as I did, I began to recognize the two figures around Ellen's bed. The man controlling Ellen was Lawson and the woman controlling me was Nico Tucker. I then noticed something else. The third figure was sitting down in a large high-backed chair. They were in complete darkness but appeared to be holding puppet controls in both hands. I looked at the strings and tried to follow them to see where the puppets were. The strings appeared to swoop upwards and were tied to two large metal rings that we're screwed into the ceiling.

I followed the strings through the metal rings and down until I realized that they were sprouting out of the top of Lawson and

Nico's heads. The puppeteer jerked them both up and down and backwards and forwards. They in turn pressed their buttons and Ellen rose and fell as I edged closer and closer in ever jerkier surges.

As I reached the door, the strip lights switched on. It was so bright that I had to shield my eyes with my hands but through my fingers, I could see that Lawson and Nico seemed to be carved from wood, their faces a macabre facsimile of their actual faces. They laughed and laughed, the sound of their voices shrill and shrieking. The puppeteer jerked them up and down more violently and as they did, the laughter got louder and louder. I wanted to put my fingers in my ears but I could no longer control my hands and just as I thought, I could stand it no longer, the strip light switched off. The room was in complete darkness, save for a spot light that seemed to be moving gradually towards the glass window. I seemed to be able to move under my own power again and so moved right up against the window. As I did so, a face suddenly appeared. It was Stella.

****

CHAPTER 16

"No. No. No. " I yelled.

Then the blackness disappeared and the light filtered in. A face loomed towards me in the light. It was The Taxi Driver.

"Wake up, you were dreaming and talking in your sleep." He said. " You weren't making any sense. "

I was relieved that none of it was real but dreams have an uncanny knack of bringing your worries to the surface. I was beginning to have trouble deciding who was to be trusted. Nico had told me that they had no intention of killing anyone but what was going to happen to Lawson or Netty or Ellen for that matter? I knew that very few things are black and white but I wasn't expecting them to be quite so grey.

"Do you know what's happened yet?" I asked the Taxi Driver

"Not yet babe. Nico and some of the others are no doubt listening to the old bill's scanners. We'll find out soon enough." He replied.

He put my blindfold back on and led me inside the bunker.

****

I was led to a chair and made to sit down before my blindfold was taken off again. The room was buzzing with activity and at the centre of it all was Nico presiding over it all like a queen bee. A number of young men and women were flitting about, passing each other notes and pulling grave faces. They were speaking in hushed voices. From time to time, they shot a sly look at The Taxi Driver and me.

"What's up with them? " I asked

"Oh, don't mind 'em. It ain't personal. Not many people are allowed in here. The Underground's centre of operations. But with Ellen and what's been happening with you, you're right in the middle of things." He said.

Nico motioned for me to approach her and as I did so, each and every one of the crowd of young people disappeared.

"Do you know what's happened with Ellen? " I asked.

"Not exactly. He police have reported a body in the hospital car park." Nico said.

I inhaled sharply

"Does that mean...?" I began to ask.

"No not necessarily." Nico cut me off. "We could only catch the word body not the sex. The signal isn't great down here. There are three possibilities. Ellen, unfortunately, Netty or Lawson. My bet is, knowing Netty, that it's most likely Lawson. Possibly Netty if he overpowered her. It's least likely to be Ellen. Netty is absolutely lethal when she's tasked with looking after someone. Especially someone as vulnerable as Ellen. It reminds her of her own best friend who was debilitated by Lawson. She's been waiting to catch up with him for a very long time."

I didn't like the idea that any one was dead. Of the three possibilities, my choice would've been Lawson and I hated myself slightly for that. What was I becoming? Nico seemed to pick up on it.

"You look thoughtful, what is it? " She said.

"I just hate all this death. It seems to follow me around at the moment." I answered.

"Yes. It follows us all around. Unfortunately, now you've decided to help us, it's likely to happen even more often. I suppose you believe that what Nemo and Co. are doing is wrong. Changing all of this vital information. Killing to keep secrets. Destroying people's lives." Nico said.

"Yes of course. But do you have to resort to the same sort of methods as they do?" I said.

Nico stared at me coldly for a long time. The room went silent and people stopped what they were doing and stared at me. I realized immediately that I'd said the wrong thing and also that I was in a vulnerable position not knowing where I was or how to escape if anything went wrong.

"Do you want to come and have a quiet chat away from everyone else?" Nico asked.

I didn't feel like I had much option.

****

CHAPTER 17

We walked down a narrow concrete corridor for about five minutes. It opened up into a large open plan room. In the corner were a number of filing cabinets.

"Drink?" Nico asked.

"Yes please." I answered but felt distinctly uneasy about it.

"Scotch, Ok? " She asked.

"Fine." I said.

Nico handed me the drink in an enamel mug and then motioned that I sat down in a worn old office chair that was placed against the back wall. It reminded me a bit of a police interrogation room which didn't help.

"You don't trust me very, much do you?" Nico said." Tell me the truth. It's always better."

I felt distinctly uncomfortable and ungrateful considering the lengths they had gone to try to look after Ellen.

"I am finding all of this really difficult. Not only that I can't believe what's happening. It seems completely unreal. I only went for a cleaning job that was so well paid it seemed too good to be true. I didn't realize that this would happen. I'm an ordinary person and so's Ellen and we've somehow walked into this massive mess. I don't know what to think and who to trust." I said.

Nico sat on her chair listening and nodding.

"I think I can understand that. How would you feel if I showed you some examples of Nemo and Co's work? Cale managed to copy some of the information before it was changed and he was assassinated. It might change your mind and you might understand better what we're trying to do here. But I warn you, it's appalling stuff. It will sicken you and if you have any compassion for others it'll make you very, very angry."

I had mixed feelings. A large part of me really didn't want to look but, I felt it was important to know. I nodded without saying anything. Nico went back to the filing cabinet and fetched a battered ring binder. She also got the bottle of scotch out for a second time. I was about to refuse but she said.

"Have another one. You'll need it."

****

There's something seductive about keeping a secret but also it can be a burden. When the secrets are lurid and despicable, the burden increases tenfold. I sat at the desk and opened the ring binder. On the inside of the first page was an index. It was split into three sections. The name of the individual who the information was about. The original information itself and then finally, the new substitute information as created by Nemo and Co. This index only documented the barest bones of the sins committed. A more in-depth version could be found in full deeper in the pages of the file. It was useful as a blackmail tool for any client who was no longer powerful or outlived their usefulness.

To begin with, the scandals involved in this book of secrets were corrupt and politically damaging but they were not so unusual. A fraud here, a bit of nepotism and a bung there. Fairly mild stuff. But as I dove deeper into the ring binder, the secrets became darker and darker. A number of very high-profile financiers and politicians involved in sex rings. Images of torture passed around by a President and his cabinet. Even a suspected serial killer as a head of state. Most of it was unbelievable but what was even more difficult to process, was the information that had been re-written and substituted in its place.

It was as though the worst bits of information about all of these powerful people had been thoroughly cleaned and disinfected.

The sex ring had become a fishing association and all of the cctv images had been doctored to reflect this new reality. I looked at the difference between the two sets of images and the pictures were extraordinary. They were flawless false versions of this alternative truth that had been created. I carried on flicking through the ring binder, comparing the two sets of information and images. They all followed the same pattern. They were so skillful that it seemed like the original truth had never existed.

"This is really shocking." I said.

"Yes." Nico agreed. " Keep reading though. It gets worse."

The last few pages were marked "Ultra Top Secret." Part of me was afraid to carry on reading as what I'd seen was bad enough. "The Black Swan Papers", was the title of this last section. The figures involved were no longer referred to by name, only a set of numbers and letters like each person had an elaborate barcode.

They all seemed to be linked but were apparently so important that they could not be associated with the consequences of what followed.

For those with top clearance only: Code Red.

"If leaked all personnel involved with "The Black Swan Papers," must deny all existence if no documentary evidence exists.

If documentary evidence does exist there are two options available.

1)Personnel must be willing to disappear without trace. Whether alive or dead there must be no paper trail. A new name is essential. Family and romantic ties must be severed. The time scale will be less than 12 hours. This option is only possible if personnel have remained entirely loyal to Nemo and Co.

2)Personnel may be terminated. If they have aligned themselves to the leak. If they show disloyalty in any way to Nemo and Co once documentary evidence has been found or seen to exist by intelligence or law enforcement agencies. Read the same for whistleblowers or infiltrators." I read.

"I'm guessing this is what happened to Cale." I said.

"Pretty much." Said Nico. "Keep on reading and you'll see why he did what he did and why we all do what we're doing."

"Contract population testing. The company has been signed up to process a number of differing tests on the population. This will not be done equitably. Certain demographics will be over represented. Others will be under represented but we need to know the effects of certain agents on these specific demographics.

1)Disease pathogens.

2)Chemical pathogens

3)Certain explosives.

4)Poisons both natural and synthetic.

Test subjects will be selected on a number of criteria which will remain secret by virtue of algorithm.

Test subjects will be unaware that they have been chosen.

Some test subjects will be given an antidote as this is the entire reason for the test.

Some test subjects will become collateral damage. There is no upper or lower limit as this is another motivation for the test.

This test has been sanctioned by multiple states and agencies. The test subjects will be selected from multiple states.

I felt as though a cold hand was gripping my throat.

"This is...?" I sputtered.

"State sanctioned genocide. In multiple countries simultaneously and on a grand scale. You see now? This is what Cale found. This is what he was killed for and this is what Stella was created to protect. She knows that we have it. But she doesn't know where we are. She knows that Cale approached you and she suspects that he was trying to get you involved." Nico said.

"But why me? This is the thing I've never been able to understand. " I said.

"You are normal and to them pretty invisible. You're the cleaner. They think you're unintelligent because of this. That you won't have the initiative or the capacity to learn the skills to disrupt what they're trying to do. They think that only they can be clever enough to deal with and manipulate this sort of information. They are both lazy and blinkered and that is to our great advantage. We can use their biases against them and prevent a terrible crime against a great number of people. If we can do it well enough, those people will wake up one morning and read it in their daily newspaper. " Nico said.

I gave a big sigh.

"I don't know how an earth I'll be able to do this." I said

"So, you will do it? " Nico smiled. It was the first time, I think, I'd ever seen it.

****

We joined the others. It was obvious that at least some had been listening as a few patted me on the back when we reappeared. Others smiled and nodded.

"So, you're back at work tomorrow. We don't have much time today to prepare you so we'll just have time to train you a bit in counter surveillance for the time being. I've a very strong feeling that our friend Lawson won't be bothering you anymore so that gives us a little more time while Stella finds another poor drone to tail you. We're going to red light another of our insiders tomorrow to create a diversion so be ready for anything. They will let you know who they are. The Taxi Driver will train you on your way home. Put the news on when you get in and keep your burner phone on. We begin tomorrow. " Nico said.

****

CHAPTER 18

As we drove back home, I tried to take in the magnitude of what I had just read. It seemed that Nemo and Co were a truly evil organization and it was all based on lies but not only lies, lies created to hide a terrible truth. To tell lies of that gravity you have to have a good memory. It's impossible to lie without one but more than that, it made me question every story I had read and every picture I'd seen. Every lie was a story, but was every story a lie?

"I'm going to put the news on. See if we can find out what's happened at the hospital." The Taxi Driver said.

The radio crackled a bit as he tuned it in.

".... Body belonged to a porter named locally as Joe Walker. Sources at the hospital say that Walker had been found acting suspiciously around a patient in the ICU and when challenged had tried to make his escape, backed against the window and fell out. The police are investigating." The newsreader said.

"That's Lawson." The Taxi Driver said." And he didn't fall."

"I didn't think so." I said.

"You don't cross, Netty." He said with a grim smile.

We carried on driving in silence for the most part. He did give me some counter surveillance tips which mostly consisted of moving around constantly and being very aware of your surroundings. Thankfully there wasn't too much of today left and I'd be having further training later. I had to be the most unlikely undercover agent.

The Taxi Driver's radio crackled into life. He spoke into it using a kind of code and then pulled over into a lay-by. I watched as he nodded and made notes. He seemed to be writing down directions vigorously. Then he quickly changed direction.

"Where are we going now?" I asked.

"To pick up Ellen. We need to go to meet Janey and swap vehicles." He said.

"Is Ellen better? " I asked.

"No but we need to move her somewhere safer until everything calms down a bit babe." He said.

"How are we going to do that? She's in intensive care!" I said "Do you have intensive care doctors and nurses in the underground as well?"

"Yes." Said The Taxi Driver looking at me as if it was a stupid question.

I'd come to the conclusion that The Underground was like an octopus. It had tentacles everywhere. I was relieved for Ellen. It was great that she would be moved out of reach of Stella and her spies. But I was afraid that we would be moving her away from one kind of danger and into another.

****

CHAPTER 19

We wove around at speed up side streets and down back alleys. I wondered if The Taxi Driver had ever been a racing driver or whether his turn of speed was just down his years of being a cabby and cutting his way through the city traffic.

It was exhilarating driving at such speeds. I intermittently looked behind to see if anyone was following us. I couldn't see anyone but it didn't mean that they weren't there. We drove for what seemed like hours until we came down a very rough track which opened out into a deserted air field. The entrance was a rusted gate that was covered with chicken wire and pad locked. There were thick verges of weeds everywhere which made it very difficult to both drive and see into the gated area. The Taxi Driver spoke into his radio and a figure came to the gate and unlocked the padlock to let us in. Once the cab had made its way through the gate, the figure padlocked it behind us and the disappeared.

We drove further along cracked Tarmac roads and passed abandoned prefabs that were covered in moss and black mould. When we got about half a mile down. I could see a fluorescent yellow vehicle covered in green writing.

"An ambulance? " I asked " Where did you get one of them from? Don't tell me. I don't think I want to know. Have you got paramedics too? "

"No." Said The Taxi Driver.

"No? Who're going to be the paramedics?" I said.

"We are." He said " What size shirt and trousers do you think you'll be?"

****

There's a feeling of power driving at very high speeds legitimately. I could see from the look on The Taxi Driver's face that he
was very much enjoying putting on the blues and twos and driving through red lights. Janey had driven off in the cab, playing
decoy once again in case Nemo and Co were trying to track us.

Though I felt in a constant state of stress or adrenaline, there
was some enjoyment to be found in this new life of intrigue. I
did suddenly feel like my life had a purpose. Having seen the
hideous potential plans that Cale Reed had uncovered had given
me a reason to get up and fight. I had doubts but what I had
read was so dreadful that I couldn't turn away from it. I, Ellen,
The Taxi Driver or Nico, any one or all of us could become one
of those test subjects. Unaware of our fate and forced into it by
dark forces beyond our control. I wasn't glad about the death of
Lawson but I was glad that Stella might find it a little bit more
difficult to track us all for a day.

Speeding through the city, I looked at all of the normal people
making their way through it oblivious to the discussions that
were happening behind closed doors. Each of those lives were
precious and important but were being weighed up against
others and decisions were being made. Most of them would
never know anything about. I hoped that it would stay that way.

****

We pulled up in to the hospital car park. The Taxi Driver spoke
into his phone and we were given directions. We were to drive
into the ambulance bay where we would be met by one of the
UR doctors and intensive care nurses. They would be bringing
Ellen with them. The plan was for the five of us to drive to a further secret location where Ellen and the medics would stay in
secret until she was well enough to be moved to the UR's head-
quarters.

As we pulled up, we realized that there was no sign of either
Ellen or the medics. I noticed that The Taxi Driver was getting

twitchy. The plan had been formulated down to the minute and those minutes were ticking by. That surely wasn't good.

"Why aren't they here?" He said in an exasperated voice. He tapped his fingers repeatedly on the steering wheel as still no one appeared. A security guard started to make his way towards us.

"Don't recognize you guys. You new? " He said.

"Yeah." Said The Taxi Driver "Just been sent over here to transfer a patient. They should be here any minute as it happens."

"Well, you can't stay parked up here for long. We need the space for other ambulances." The security guard said.

I could see he was really irritating The Taxi Driver.

"If they're not here in five minutes. We'll drive round and come back." Said The Taxi Driver.

The security guard pulled a face and walked off shaking his head.

"Berk." Said The Taxi Driver. "If they're not here in two minutes I'm going to see if I can page them. They should've been here five minutes ago.

Just as he got his pager out, I heard an almighty crash. I spun around and looked out of the window. A car and a transit van had collided into each other. The security guard went running off towards them and the drivers of the two vehicles got out and started remonstrating with each other.

"Look sharp." The Taxi Driver said and nodded towards the front windscreen. I could see a doctor and nurse moving towards us pushing a gurney with Netty bringing up the rear.

"Out you get and let 'em in." The Taxi Driver said.

I got out unsure whether to walk or run but decided that walking looked less suspicious. I opened up the back doors of the ambulance just as the gurney arrived and once, I'd moved the platform down, managed to help them get Ellen secured in

place ready to go. Netty winked at me and moved off quickly
back into the hospital. I noticed as I put my seat belt on, that the
security guard was making his way towards the ambulance.

"Bloody hell, what does he want now?" said The Taxi Driver.

"What did you say your patients name was?" Asked the security
guard.

"I didn't. Listen mate, we need to get going. We're late as it is."
The Taxi Driver was starting to get angry.

"Well, I don't think you are who you say you are." Said the security guard and started to reach into his jacket.

I didn't comprehend at first what was happening. I didn't see the
gun or notice the bullet ricocheting towards the windscreen.
The Taxi Driver put his foot down and accelerated towards the
security guard who kept trying shoot at the ambulance that
was rapidly moving towards him. I ducked down away from the
bullets that intermittently peppered the windscreen. The Taxi
Driver kept driving forwards. Suddenly the shooting stopped
and there was a sickening crash. I saw the security guard hit the
windscreen and bounced off the bonnet. I didn't see what happened next, I just heard a terrible screeching noise and a number
of bumps.

I froze in my seat. I could hear a faint tapping behind my seat
and muffled voices who sounded like they were asking what
was going on. The Taxi Driver said nothing, put the sirens on and
kept driving.

****

CHAPTER 20

The rest of our journey stayed largely silent. I looked at the Taxi Driver. His face didn't give anything away. How did he feel? Had he just killed a man? I suspected it wasn't the first time and how did he live with it? I looked at this arm and noticed that at least one of the bullets had hit its target. The blood seeped through his paramedic's shirt and trickled down his arm. He didn't seem to notice. He seemed oblivious to anything but the curve of the road which he stuck to swiftly and expertly. I looked at his face and noticed a tear trickling down his face.

"He was one of theirs babe." He said. " Don't make it right but he was one of theirs."

I could only nod along and touch his hand.

****

We pulled up to a large but unassuming house in the suburbs. It was gated and surrounded by a high fence on one side and a hedge from the other. It would be very difficult to see inside the garden from the road. The entire street was in darkness and was only lit by the pale blue light of the moon.

The Taxi Driver made what seemed to be a tense call, the content of which I couldn't decipher very well as it seemed to be in code.

"I'm in the doghouse, babe. We'll get Ellen sorted. Then I've got to see Nico. I've drawn unwanted attention to us so am gonna have to go to ground for a while." He said.

"I'm not sure you had a lot of choice. It was self-defense and he could've killed all of us." I said

"Yes, Nico knows that too but it means I could have a bit of a target on my back if any of Stella's goons have been able to work out who was driving the ambulance from the cctv." He said.

"Do you think they will have been able to see either of us? If so, surely, it'd be pretty hard for me to spy in the office? " I said.

"Well let's hope the camera in the car park wasn't working or the picture was a bit grainy." He said.

A side door opened a figure beckoned and the doctor and nurse pulled the gurney and machinery into the building. Ellen was still unconscious. I was amazed that she hadn't been awakened by all of the drama that was going on around her. I hoped that she was going to be ok. I felt awful for including her in all of this. It didn't seem fair at all.

The hallway opened up into a large room with medical machinery ready for Ellen to be hooked up to. I was amazed that the UR had all of this equipment ready at their disposal.

"Is this always here? " I asked The Taxi Driver.

"Yes. The Underground needs somewhere to bring people. It serves as a safe house as well as a medical centre. People don't always need treatment but having the threat of Nemo and Co. hanging over many of us means that it isn't always safe for us to go to the local hospital." He said.

I couldn't help but wonder where all of the money would come from to pay for a place like this. Up until now, I hadn't thought of the underground as being a particularly well-off organization. It certainly had a network of supporters in a lot of very useful places, today's situation with Ellen had proven that. But you needed serious money to be able to afford the sort of equipment stored here.

I had to ask.

"Who pays for all this?"

"The Underground does." The Taxi Driver said.

"Yes, but how? It isn't a few sponsored walks and a bake sale is it?" I said.

"I couldn't tell you, babe honestly. Nico's in charge of all of that stuff. Cale knew but obviously he ain't around no more, God bless him. We're only told on a need-to-know basis and most of us don't need to know. I wouldn't bother love honestly; I don't think Nico would be into anything dodgy." He said.

I was hoping he was right but something kept nagging at me. There was more to it than met the eye, I was sure of it.

****

CHAPTER 21

Everything was moving so slowly. I could see the man's face, bloodied and battered in the windscreen. He was just laid there, staring hard with unseeing eyes. There were spider cracks in the glass and he just appeared to get nearer and nearer. The glass shattered and his left arm and hand broke through the glass and grasped my hand in an iron grip.

He leered closer and pulled my hand through the hole in the glass. He pulled it hard until we were eyeball to eyeball against the screen. He mouthed something that I couldn't make out at first. His mouth opened and closed like a goldfish as his tongue lolled between his teeth. I realized that he was mouthing the word "Killer" over and over again.

I looked at the seat next to me. There was no sign of the Taxi Driver, just an empty seat and a pool of blood that had accumulated to the side of where he'd been sat. I could see his outline, but he himself had disappeared.

Suddenly the ambulance stopped. The security guard also disappeared. I got out of the ambulance and went to the back doors and opened them. There was no one inside, merely the gurney and heart monitor which was flatlining loudly and constantly. As I stepped out of the ambulance, I could see the outline of thousands and thousands of figures. They had no faces at all, merely outlines and they stretched all the way back to the horizon and beyond. A strong wind started to blow and I could hear a loud fluttering sounding like the wings of many birds soaring and diving in the sky. But there weren't any birds just lots of sheets of paper floating down from the heavens. They covered the floor like snow. Each one read exactly the same thing. Acceptable collateral damage. Acceptable collateral damage.

****

Day 7

I didn't remember getting home. Once we'd made sure Ellen was safe and comfortable, I'd fallen asleep. I'd had some vague memory of being lifted into bed. I half expected waking up in the bunker or with The Taxi Driver sitting on the settee. I wondered how long it would be until I saw him again. I'd got quite used to him in the end.

I checked my usual phone. No messages. It was almost too quiet. It felt weird to be getting no messages from Ellen but the fact that Stella hadn't sent any either unnerved me.

I stepped out of the front door at three am and noticed a black cab. It flashed its lights at me. I approached it with a sense of trepidation. I knew it was very unlikely to be the Taxi Driver after yesterday.

"Wanna lift to work?" A familiar voice said.

I looked in the driver's seat. It was Janey.

****

I arrived at the Nemo and Co. office at 3.55 sharp. Janey dropped me off and with a wave, she was gone. I hadn't found anything out about what had happened to the Taxi Driver or where he'd gone. It seemed Janey was my new bodyguard, or the time being at least.

I walked to the door and it opened automatically. I expected to hear Stella's voice but there was only an eerie silence. I walked towards the office and instead of the darkness, I was used to, it was lit with a pale blue light.

The left-hand door opened and I saw the office was as usual. Rows and rows of empty desks and my cleaning cart in the corner.

Because I hadn't received any instructions from Stella, I just went to the cart and started to clean. There seemed to be no power at all feeding into the computers, not even the stand by lights were flickering. I wondered what other information was secreted inside these terminals buried in all of those zeros and ones. I had a fierce urge to pick up the mop handle and smash it into the screens, knock as many of the laptops onto the floor as I could but I realized the information would still exist, elsewhere. In another laptop.

"So, you're here?" The metallic voice was unmistakable. " With your friend's accident I wasn't sure you would be. It is so difficult when our loved ones are hurt isn't it?" Stella said.

Part of me wanted to scream at her. How would she know being a metal psychopath? How many automatons have friends or loved ones?

But I sensed she was trying to put out feelers. Maybe even psyche me out. I wasn't prepared to go along with that, especially after what I'd read.

"What do you know about that? " I said, wondering if she would admit to spying or try to concoct a story to try to explain things.

"I know your address of course and read about it in the newspaper. Poor Ellen. So difficult when you've lived a life of disappointment and then the loss of a dream job. It can be so damaging." Stella said.

I knew then that she was definitely trying to push my buttons. I was so angry; I was tempted to make some dry quip about Lawson. But I couldn't. I hadn't liked him or his spying but he didn't deserve to die. He seemed to be a pawn of circumstance just like the rest of us.

"I'd quite like to get on if I could. You're right that it's been a difficult few days, but I can get on if I'm just left to work." I said.

I tried to keep cleaning and ignore Stella's menacing presence. I couldn't see her but knew she was still there, observing and taking notes. As I made my way around the room, in the corner of my eye I could see a silvery glint highlighted in the cold blue light. It was the chrome outline of a female automaton. She seemed as a mirage shimmering in the desert sun. The fact that I could only make out the faintest of outlines seemed to amplify her malicious presence. She was far taller than I imagined. Seven feet at least, I estimated, as the top of her head almost grazed the ceiling. Her burnished chrome limbs were sleek and powerful and she appeared to have a number of thick metallic wires sprouting out from the top of her head. They appeared to have a life of their own and undulated like eels. Being alone with her in the semi darkness was frightening. I could see she had the power to tear me to pieces if she wanted. Yet I was strangely fascinated. I was wary of turning my back on her, fearing she would be at my shoulder within seconds.

"Do send Ellen my best wishes." She said " If you can find her."

I turned to face the outline and she'd gone. I hadn't heard a sound as she disappeared. It was terrifying.

****

CHAPTER 22

The rest of the shift had passed without any further incident. Some workers had appeared, checking information, deleting and typing. I moved around them quietly, unnoticed, wondering how I'd be able to help the underground. Was I so invisible that I'd be able to spirit away the information Nico Tucker needed without any of the workers or Stella becoming aware of it? I wasn't so sure. I looked at my watch. I thought that Nico must've decided against causing a distraction after all. It was almost ten o' clock and I made my way to the corner of the room with the cleaning trolley ready to leave it in its usual place.

Just as I did so there was an extremely loud noise and a low rumble that reverberated around the room and knocked me to the ground.

"What the hell was that? " I said out loud not expecting any one to answer. The light went from blue to red and an alarm began to blare from a number of invisible speakers. I felt a figure rush by and drop something next to my right shoe. They stopped running for a split second and looked at me full in the face. They were a member of the underground. I looked down and saw a USB stick. I knelt as if to tie my shoelace and popped it into my shoe.

The figure looked at me with the faint glimmer of a smile, started to run again and I quietly disappeared. As I made my way down the corridor towards the exit, I felt a powerful rush of air that pinned me to the wall. I shut my eyes as it passed but then opened them again with just enough time to see the faintest glint of chrome flying down the corridor in front of me like molten mercury.

I knew, I needed to leave quickly and get out. As I opened the door, I saw Janey's cab parked up at the other side of the road. But between us was the body of the man I had just seen at the office. The same man who had dropped the USB stick at my feet. He'd created a diversion and paid with his life for doing it. As for Stella, there was no sign of her anywhere. It was like she was a figment of my imagination.

****

I handed the USB to Janey. No words passed between us. I really wanted to ask her how The Taxi Driver was but I wasn't sure she would know or that she would tell me if she did.

"We need to visit Nico. " She said. " Put your blindfold on love and have a sleep, you've earned it."

I put the scarf around my eyes and felt. I couldn't agree less. I was so tired, I vaguely heard Janey on the phone to the police and ambulance but drifted off before I could hear the end of the conversation.

****

"You did well. " Nico said.

I couldn't see. Everything was black but then I realized that I hadn't taken the blindfold off.

"I'm not so sure about that." I said. "A man died."

"He knew the risks and he was happy to take them. His girlfriend was killed by Nemo and Co. so he was willing to do what he could to help. You got the USB stick with the new information, that's what you were asked to do. It was very important and you got it out of the building without being caught or killed. Pretty good for a beginner." Nico smiled.

I was bothered by how little she seemed to acknowledge the man's death but also how many of the members of the underground seemed to have dead or injured loved ones. Nico had spoken about my lack of trust in our last meeting, she wasn't wrong. The appalling information uncovered by Cale Reed was the best reason to try to disrupt the operations of Nemo and Co. But it didn't mean that Nico's methods were totally legitimate either. I wondered if vulnerable people were being recruited when they didn't really have the capacity to say no.

"What information is there on the USB stick?" I asked, fairly sure that she wouldn't tell me.

"More plans for the population experiments mainly. It's quite vague and in code so they are further down the line but nothing seems imminent in the next week. I'll need to get some of the code breakers involved. You need to get some sleep. I'll leave you to it for a couple more hours."

And with that she disappeared out of the door.

****

Day 8

When I came round eventually, I realized that I must've slept at the bunker. I sat up and saw I wasn't in my own bed, but in a spartan metal single bed much like those found in prisons or an army barracks. There was a single wardrobe with no clothes in there and the walls were bare concrete. Not very inspiring. I found that I had no idea where I was or indeed if there were any one else there. I didn't know if it was day or night and where I could find any food or drink. I didn't even know where the toilet was.

I felt groggy and decided to look around to see if I could find anyone. I opened the door and found myself in a narrow corridor peppered with a number of doors at either side. I walked up to the first one and tried to open it but it was locked. I walked up to the next one which was also locked. I tried each and every door along the corridor, everyone was locked. I looked up at the ceiling and I heard a low buzzing sound. At first, I thought the buzzing was coming from the blinking ceiling lights but it seemed to grow louder the further I moved away from them.

I came to a pair of double doors at the end of the corridor. They were old and worn, with peeling red paint that seemed to flake off in clumps and settle in heaps on the floor. These doors were open and I pushed my way through them. I found myself walking down an identical corridor but this time the doors were open. I could hear the buzzing getting louder and louder.

I peered around the first door. In the corner of the room was a seated figure. I shouted over to them but they didn't reply. They had their back to me. I called again and again they didn't reply. As I moved closer, I saw they were wearing a black jacket which appeared to be moving and breathing. I got closer still and saw that the jacket wasn't black at all. It was swarming with blowflies.

I ran out of the room and down the corridor to the next room where there was another figure sat on a chair with the back to the door. The buzzing carried on getting louder. I kept on running to the next room and the next. Every time I opened the door, I saw the same sight. I decided I needed to get out of the corridor and away from the bunker and somehow get back home. But how could I when I had no idea where I was?

Once again at the end of the corridor, I could see some red double doors. I tried to run but my feet kept sticking to the floor. The harder I tried to move forward the more I remained stuck. I looked down and saw what appeared to be blood on the floor. Suddenly, I came to the double doors and concluded that the blood was emanating from there. I found myself propelled forward by a power that wasn't my own. I was in a large hall with a stage at the back and sat in the middle of it, was an ambulance. The windscreen was sprayed with a constellation of bullet holes. There were two figures inside the ambulance, neither appeared to be moving. Gingerly, I moved forward and as I did the floodlights came up and illuminated the ambulance.

I climbed the stairs at the side of the stage and moved towards the side window of the ambulance. I saw The Taxi Driver and security guard sat side by side. They were both wearing paramedics uniforms and had wounds in their faces and arms. I called out but then looked down at myself and realized that I was wearing a security guards' uniform. I also felt something cold in my hand. It was a hand gun. I felt the panic rise in my throat and all I could do was run away as fast as I could, to I didn't know where. As I did, I caught sight of my reflection in a pane of glass. There was a small, red circle right in the middle of my forehead.

****

CHAPTER 23

When I finally woke up, it took a couple of minutes before I knew where I was. I was feeling slightly groggy still but saw I was in my own bed. I had no recollection of how I got there. My two phones were on the bed side table. Neither one was blinking with unanswered messages. I ran my fingers across my forehead just to check that I hadn't actually got a wound there. I was relieved to note that there wasn't one.

What was worrying though was how bizarre things seemed to keep happening and I wasn't sure who was responsible for it. It seemed that either Nemo and Co. or The UR could be the culprit. I'd never had so many weird dreams. Was it just a way of coming to terms with all of the trauma or was something more sinister happening? I couldn't know for sure. I wished that I had Ellen to talk to. I wondered how she was being looked after in the UR's safe house. It almost felt unreal, like I'd imagined it all. I often wished, I had.

****

"The death of a security guard working at Brigdale hospital has been classified as murder. The police are seeking a couple falsely posing as paramedics. They are also wanted in connection with the kidnapping of a patient and two members of staff." The newsreader said.

I looked incredulously at the TV.

"That is such bullshit." I shouted.

"It seems that the couple stole an ambulance and then drove off whilst James Gordon, 36 attempted to confront them. They drove on, running him over in the process."

I couldn't believe what I was hearing. Nothing in the report was true other than the Taxi Driver and I were falsely posing as paramedics. We had taken Ellen out of the hospital but it was to protect her.

I heard my burner phone ping. A message had come through. It was from Nico.

"Are you watching the news?" It read. "They are starting to rewrite what happened. They cannot work out who you are from the CCTV but don't be surprised by anything that happens in the next few days. Be on high alert."

What does that even mean? I thought. I could see why the Taxi Driver had gone to ground but then he'd also been at all this longer than me.

"How's Ellen? " I replied. "Can I come to visit her again soon?"

Another text pinged in quick reply.

"She's fine. But give it a few days. We'll see how things pan out."

I wasn't really happy about it but could see the sense in it. I didn't like the fact that Ellen was all alone, in God knows where being looked after by people she didn't know. I wished I could be there but didn't want to put her in any further danger than she was actually in.

I turned back to the TV. Reading the ticker tape strip at the bottom of the screen, it seemed that someone was well and truly rewriting what had happened to the security guard. It was disconcerting to see it happening in real time and through the TV. One of the CCTV stills pictures flashed up. The security guard's body had been blurred. I saw that it was impossible to see who was actually sat in either the driver's or passenger's seat of the ambulance through the window. I wondered if there were already some manipulations underway to make sure that some fall guy or girl of choice would end up as a convenient patsy for Nemo and Co. on the 9'O clock news.

"James Gordon's family are saluting a fallen hero tonight, who gave his life in order to save a patient he didn't even know. But as his family report that was just in his nature." Said the newsreader nodding gravely.

Pictures flashed up of a news conference filled to the brim with reporters. A young woman, probably not much older than thirty, addressed the camera. She elaborated on his heroism, how they'd only recently become parents and that he'd loved his job. If I hadn't been there at the time and actually experienced what had happened, I would've been taken in too. But the level of detail involved in this rewriting both sickened and fascinated me in equal measure. I wondered who James Gordon's wife was. Was she really his wife? Or was she an actress who'd been hired specially to play the part? Was she just another employee? Did they really have a child or was this all part of the story telling? Was the security guard really called James Gordon? Did he approve of Nemo and Co? Did he even know how they actually operated or was he merely another cog in the operation who had no idea what all the other cogs did? Would he have altered his life if he did know?

I realized that I didn't trust many of the things I saw or read anymore. I had never really questioned the news before. I understood that facts were spun sometimes but certainly not completely erased or substituted with alternative details. I saw that this could have been going on for years and the things I took for granted were not as immovable as I once thought. At that moment, I felt as though the ground beneath my feet shifted slightly and I fell head first into a black hole.

****

CHAPTER 24

Being a suspect in a concocted murder was a novel experience. I didn't like it and now that The Taxi Driver had disappeared to some unknown location, I didn't have anyone I trusted around to share it with. I liked Janey but didn't know her yet. Ellen was in the safe house and Nico Tucker for all her zeal, didn't seem to be a sympathetic ear. I also wasn't entirely sure that she didn't harbour cruelties of her own. She was quite rightly devoted to protecting people from the appalling policies that Nemo and Co were served to cover up but I sensed another motivation, not only that of revenge for Cale Reed's death. There was more to it but what at that stage I didn't know.

I was also concerned about what had happened to The Taxi Driver. Had he disappeared for his own protection or had he been vanished because he'd caused trouble for The Underground and deviated from Nico's plans. I had no way of knowing until he appeared again. Dead or alive. I hoped it was the latter, but I was afraid it was the former.

****

The doorbell rang. I wasn't expecting it and blearily looked at the alarm clock to see that it was still very early. I picked up the entry phone. It was Janey.

"Would you be ready to come to see Ellen? Then we've got to go see Nico for your next assignment. Next one's a bit more involved, I think. I'll be downstairs. Don't be long."

As I made my way downstairs, my phone pinged.

"Not now. Not now." I thought.

I looked at the message. It was Stella.

"Don't come to the office tomorrow. Your shift has been cancelled. You'll be needed as usual on Friday. You will be paid for tomorrow as usual. "

Another ping and a notification that I'd been paid came through.

Bit weird, I thought. There was no explanation for my shift being cancelled. Had Nemo and Co. discovered that I had been travelling in the ambulance when James Gordon had been killed or was there another explanation?

****

The roads were deserted as we set off. Janey made small talk as we drove through main roads and back streets. I looked out of the window and was amazed how quiet the streets were.

"So, are you enjoying being an outlaw?" Janey asked.

"Not really. I wish it had never happened. I wish all of it had never happened. I'm not quite sure how I found myself in the situation. I'm just a normal person. I don't have the skills for this or the memory. I don't know why Nico wants me to do all of this so badly. Why me? Why me?" I shouted.

I hadn't acknowledged quite how stressful this situation had become. I suppose I had stuffed it all down and it had only really come out in my dreams.

"I'm sorry love." Janey said. " Nothing really prepares you for all of this. I can't explain why Nico chose you specifically. Obviously because you work there it helps but she probably also sees something in you that maybe you don't see yourself yet."

"I'm worried about Ellen and your brother. Is he ok? " I said.

"I'm pretty sure he is. He's big enough and hairy enough to look after himself. But he's been here before so try not to fret pet, ok" Janey said.

"What happened, can you tell me?" I asked.

"Sure, what I know about it. You know how he got involved with The Underground and why?" Janey asked.

"I know why he joined." I said.

"Well one day Cale flagged down his cab and spoke to him about what The Underground were trying to do. You didn't really meet Cale, did you? "

"No apart from the time on the bus when he tried to recruit me just before he was killed. "

"He was a really nice fella. " said Janey " If Nico is the brains of the outfit you could say that Cale was the heart. He was less interested in the ideology of things. He just cared about people and he treated my brother a bit like a second Dad and that really helped him. He also was originally Cale's bodyguard and driver before he was yours. In fact, if he hadn't been called away on a job, Cale would never have got on that second bus. Cale had told him not to worry because a trusted friend of his had phoned him and told him he could get on the bus. I guess you don't know that the not in service busses are clandestine transport for Nemo and Co. workers. Cale thought he was safe going on there because his friend, the man who blew both of them and the bus up, was working for Nemo and Co and the Underground too. Unfortunately, though, it seems like his loyalties were not ultimately to the Underground. My brother was incensed when he knew what had happened. He would've killed the culprit if he wasn't already dead. He was absolutely livid and Nico knew that so she made sure that he had a new job to do to look after you and Ellen. Anyway, I digress.

Years ago, before all of this existed, my brother was working in the Middle East undercover for some outfit. He didn't or couldn't tell me on what at the time. There had been a high-profile politician murdered in some seedy backstreet brothel. It had emerged that this politician was involved in all manner of corruption and dodgy dealings. This outfit obviously had links to the politician but something somewhere along the line had gone wrong, whether they had meant to kill him or protect him was never established. Later, my brother told me that he'd been out eating and noticed on a news bulletin that this politician had been murdered.

At that point he was concerned about what was happening but by the time he reached home and turned the TV on his own picture was being used as he was being set up as the prime suspect."

"It's awful. And now it's happening again." I said.

"Yes but at least he's had that experience and he knows what to do. He also has some back up this time and hasn't been hung out to dry like he was before so, it's not all bad. " Janey said

I was grateful to Janey. There was something very calming about her. She seemed very unruffled and practical. She helped give me some confidence that in the midst of all of this chaos, that everything would be ok in the end. I did find it strange though that she hadn't mentioned Jane at all. i had no idea why.

As we drove out of the centre of the city, I put my blindfold on and listened to the sounds of the tires on different parts of the road. After a while it was obvious which parts had been newly resurfaced and which were covered with a patchwork of Tarmac and exposed concrete. The cab hummed and vibrated as it made its way towards the suburbs. With every short stop at the traffic lights the breaks squealed as they were applied quite suddenly. Then as the engine got back up to speed, it sounded like a pair of great lungs were releasing a breath.

I was amazed how little I could hear other vehicles. Even that early, they usually swarmed the roads like ants but it was eerily quiet. Still. There was something unnatural about the quietness.

We soon arrived at the safe house. Janey helped me out of the cab and led me to a pair of metal gates which clanked loudly as they closed behind us. It felt a bit weird being blindfolded here having driven here in the dark without one but I'd had no idea where we were in the dark and the further, I became involved with The Underground, there was a large part of me who wanted to know as little as possible. With so much of the infor-

115

mation being apparently dangerous it made sense to distance myself from it as much as possible.

We kept walking for a few minutes through what felt like a narrow corridor and then back outside into a small building that was next to the main house. As we got inside, Janey helped me take my blindfold off. I saw Ellen in her bed still hooked up to the various machinery that was tasked with keeping her alive. I was sad to see she still needed them but her wounds definitely showed signs of healing. I started to feel a sense of hope, that Ellen just might recover and was being kept safe here.

"Can I sit with her for a minute?" I asked the nurse who hovered in the background keeping watch.

He nodded in agreement and I sat in the chair next to Ellen's bed and held her hand.

"You've got about ten minutes before we need to set off again, love. I'll wait outside for you. Give you a bit of time alone." Janey said and went outside and closed the door quietly behind her.

I pulled up the chair more closely to Ellen's bed.

"Oh Ellen. I hope you can hear me. I've so much I'd like to tell you but I can't at the moment. I want to apologize to you. I've involved you in something that has put you in danger. I didn't mean to because I didn't know I had done." I said and the tears fell down my face in streams.

"You're my best friend and I would never do anything to hurt you on purpose. I just really want you to wake up and when you do, I don't want you to worry about where you are. I'm sorry you aren't at home and you won't recognize anyone around you either but they're here to look after you and keep you safe. I'll come back to see you when I can."

I snuffled into my hand. I felt like I was abandoning her and hated it. The Nurse patted my shoulder.

"She is getting there you know and am pretty sure she can hear you. We'll do our best for her and will make sure you know when she wakes up." He said.

I just nodded and walked out of the door putting my blindfold on as I left. Janey grabbed my arm and squeezed it.

****

CHAPTER 25

For the rest of the journey, I stayed silent. I felt completely exhausted. Janey sung away to herself and tapped the steering wheel in time. I rested my head against the side of the cab and found myself vibrating backwards and forwards in time with the falling and rising of the undulating road. I felt drowsy with the movement but was determined to stay awake as I didn't want another nightmare. They were happening too often. Seeing the dead faces of those victims of Nemo and Co., weaving in front of my eyes were terrible reminders of the unfair exchange that people such as Cale Reed had made. Their lives for the keeping of other people's secrets. Secrets that didn't deserve to be kept. Even the security guard would still be alive if those secrets weren't be kept and the information erased. He was also a victim of theirs in another way.

Aside from all of that, I was afraid of seeing Ellen's face in my dreams. Being angry, accusing me of betraying her. Who knows, maybe even hating me for drawing her in, even though I hadn't meant to. But in a sense Ellen couldn't accuse me or hate me more than I did myself at that moment. I had this heavy knot of dread that seemed to live constantly in my stomach. It was like my own dark secret and I couldn't rewrite it.

****

The journey to the bunker had become familiar. Even with the blindfold on, each step towards the central hall had become ingrained in my memory. I began to think that after a while blindfolds must become redundant because each of the other senses become heightened. I recognized the slightly damp mouldy smell of concrete; I could almost see the green moss coagulating on the ceiling. There was the sound of dripping water and the splash of puddles on my boot as I tramped through. Each step ground against the floor, but I could feel the small pebbles underneath my rubber boot.

For such a large building, I was amazed at how quiet it was. All of the underground volunteers seemed to walk around in relative silence. There was no conversation buzzing with ideas. Any talking appeared to be conducted in whispers. I wondered if people had problems trusting each other, like I did. Were they fearful of Nico? And if so why? Were there things going on under the surface that I didn't know about. I felt Janey's reassuring grip on my arm as she steered me towards the hall and the hard wood of the chair as I sat down.

"I've got some important things to tell you. There was a secret file on the USB stick. Thankfully our hacking experts were able to get into it. I'm afraid our worst fears have been realized." Nico said.

I shuddered slightly, afraid of what she was going say. I suddenly saw that Janey had disappeared and only Nico and I remained in the hall alone.

"Did you receive a text from Nemo and Co. asking you not to go in tomorrow?" Nico said.

"Yes, I did. I thought it was weird." I said . "How did you know? " I asked.

"In the USB it mentions that one of the population experiments are going to be carried out tomorrow but doesn't mention what form it could take. We've got a few plans ready but we can't plan for every scenario. All members of The Underground have been called up and are on high alert ready to support the community the best way that we can." Nico spoke gravely.

I had an awful cold feeling in my veins. Having read the Nemo and Co. plans, I knew all the scenarios were terrible. I wasn't sure what anyone could do to prevent the worst of them.

"Do you know anything at all about what's going to happen? " I asked.

"Only that it will happen within the city and up to the suburbs. That's why we think you've been asked not to go in. We don't know if they're expecting you to have died or if they just don't want you around while the worst of the rewriting goes on." Nico said.

The brutality of it hit me between the eyes.

"They really don't give a shit about anyone do they? " I said.

"No. Normal people are of very little value. Just economic units or organisms to be experimented on. The sad thing is any results will be saved to merely further their influence, not to help anyone." Nico said.

I felt rooted to the spot. Any of the nightmares I'd had recently paled into significance compared to the reality that was unfolding in front of me.

"What are you going to do?" I asked.

"First we need to evacuate as many members of the underground from the designated area as possible. That includes Ellen, Netty and family members. If we have enough room here to accommodate other members of the public we will do. That of course means you'll need to sleep here over night in one of the dormitories." Nico said.

"But I haven't got any of my stuff. " I said.

"Don't worry, we've got everything you could need here. We can send for your possessions later if it's safe or you need them. We don't know how long we'll be here. It could be overnight or it could be months." Nico said.

"Months? Why on earth could we be here for months? What on earth could they do that would mean we had to be here for months" I said

"A virus? Radioactive waste? I hope it won't be necessary to stay here that long but if you need to, you can." Nico said. " I'll ask Janey to take you to your room and I'll let you know a bit more in the morning."

With that, Nico left. She seemed to disappear into the corner of the room. Janey emerged at my shoulder with a bag. My name was stenciled on the front of it.

"These are for you love. Some clobber in there. They ain't very trendy but they'll keep you going for a couple of days. " Janey said.

I took the bag and followed Janey down a dark corridor. There were a few blinking caged lights in the ceiling, it made it difficult to see more than a few feet in front of or behind us. I could feel that we were moving deeper underground as the floor sloped downwards under our feet.

As we reached the bottom of the corridor, there was a thick wooden door. It was open and I noticed a bunk bed in the left-hand corner of what was a small windowless room.

"Will anyone else be sleeping in here? "I asked.

Janey shrugged.

"Dunno babe. I suppose it depends how many people evacuate here. Nico's got me driving around the city for the rest of the day picking people up. I don't think we'll know until tonight. I'll probably see you later. "She said.

After she'd gone, I opened the bag to see what was in there. Perfectly folded shirt and trousers in black. I noticed that there was an underground logo stenciled on the pocket in red. It reminded me of a guerrilla uniform. It was a strange choice of spare clothing. I also found a tooth brush and wash cloth which also featured a UR logo embroidered on it. The UR really are a brand, aren't they? I thought which seemed really ironic. I rooted further into the bag and found a couple of books. One was just a large pulpy thriller, the sort of book you read when you're on holiday somewhere hot. The second was a large A4 sized note-

book with The UR logo on the front and the title,
"The Manifesto" stenciled in red letters.

"What does that even mean?" I thought. I decided to lay down on
the bed and try to relax, though the room wasn't really comfortable in any way. As, I lay there I noticed a further few details of
my surroundings. Fixed to the wall above the door, was a TV set.
It was an ancient model and because I couldn't see a remote or
on/off button, I wasn't convinced that it even worked.

I also saw a small speaker fitted into the wall. Once again it
seemed old and decrepit and I wondered whether this would
be the means that Nico would impart information or make demands.

The last thing I noticed was there was no clock on the wall so
without a phone or watch, it was impossible to know what time
it was. This could be very disorientating considering there were
no windows or natural light. I was thankful that I had my watch
in my coat pocket. My gut instinct was telling me to keep it hidden and not let on that I had it at all.

"Can everyone come out of their rooms and walk down the corridor to the central hall? We'll have a meeting, there are important things to discuss, then we'll eat." Nico's voice fed through
the speakers. It had a tinny quality that almost reminded me of
Stella.

****

CHAPTER 26

I opened the door and there stood Janey outside. She was dressed in an UR uniform, just like the one I'd been given in my bag.

"You not wearing yours?" She asked.

"Not till my clothes are dirty." I said " I don't like uniforms."

Janey shrugged and we walked together in silence towards the central hall. We walked in and I was astounded to see hundreds of people gathered. All wearing UR uniforms. It appeared that I was the only one who wasn't. I looked around the crowd to see if there was anyone that I recognized. Near the front, I could see Netty and as I looked a bit further back, I noticed a man who looked like The Taxi Driver but there was something different about him. I tried to wave but he didn't seem to see me.

I looked on to the stage where I noticed a podium had been erected with microphones and a large UR logo that was printed on a large square of black cloth. Nico appeared in the spotlight, seemingly reveling in the loud round of applause that greeted her. I looked around me at all of the faces studying her with rapt attention. It reminded me of a political rally, which seemed very weird under the circumstances. I zoned out as I really felt uncomfortable at what was going on. All of these people were supposed to be being protected here from an event designed to harm them and yet all of a sudden, it didn't feel like that.

"As you know, we are all here for an important purpose. The most important purpose. To save humanity from those who may wish to destroy it." Nico began to speak in a rousing fashion, banging on the podium to emphasize the important words or phrases.

"They may present themselves as the saviours of democracy or of a certain way of life, but we know that that is a work of fiction that misrepresents what it is that these traitors actually do."

A great cheer went up. Each figure clapped and cheered the end of every phrase. With each round of applause, Nico grew in stature looking across the crowd almost imperiously as they roared and clapped in unison.

I felt as if I was completely alone. As if everyone else were joined together in one huge private joke and I was the only one who didn't get it.

"Tomorrow, this devilish company and their masters in various governments will unleash a torrent of destruction which will condemn countless ordinary citizens to possible death, disability or destitution.

At this moment, we do not know what method they will employ. We do know however that we will use whatever means necessary to stop them from carrying out their plan."

I looked around at the people around me. They seemed blank faced, even dead behind the eyes. Their reactions seemed unnatural, orchestrated even. As Nico continued to talk, she roused them into more fervent reactions and yet they seemed as though they were hypnotized and not reacting on their own power. I wondered if they had been drugged or if it was one massive shared delusion. There was an undercurrent of rage buzzing around that hall. I felt a bit like I had to pretend to go along with it for my own safety. It felt as though the atmosphere was imbued with a subtle kind of menace, a sense of ultra-conformity that wasn't to be stood up against.

The irony was not lost on me that this organisation that wanted quite rightly to protect people didn't seem to want to encourage differences in outlook or opinion.

"When you go back to your rooms, I want you to read your copy of the manifesto. It is to be your Bible. It sets out very graphically what is expected from you in order to dismantle the hideous sore that Nemo and Co. have become and what we need to do to replace it.

You must follow each recommendation to the letter. It may be that you will be asked to make the ultimate sacrifice as our fellow resister, Sean Hayes was asked to do just a few days ago."

There was another round of cheering and applause. A lot of words were cropping up in Nico's speech that I was uncomfortable with. I couldn't wait to get out of there and get back into my bedroom. I wondered where Ellen was and what on earth, she would make of all of this. I was reminded of a news report I'd watched about a doomsday cult who all ended up committing suicide on bunk beds wearing new white trainers because they thought they were going to be taken up by a comet. I didn't want that to be us but I was becoming afraid that that was the sort of thing Nico wanted.

****

I hadn't sat down to eat with so many people at one time since eating school dinners. The food tasted pretty similar too. I thought they must've been planning this for a very long time. To find this amount of food is not something that happens overnight. I kept scanning the faces. They were all ages, creeds and colours. I wondered how Nico and Cale had managed to recruit them. Were they all grieving relatives vulnerable and wanting revenge or were some of them idealists who wanted a better world, who didn't agree with how unfair life often is and wanted to redress the balance? Did some of them just enjoy a fight, with fire in their bellies moving from one cause to another.? Or did they simply believe that what they were doing was the right and moral thing to do? I wondered if there were anyone else like me who didn't really know why they were there at all and were shouldering a heavy sense of doubt. If they agreed that what Nemo and Co. were planning was wrong but they also had deep misgivings about the methods used by the UR. If there was anyone else who felt like that, they didn't show it.

The atmosphere had changed now people were eating as people laughed and joked together and the febrile atmosphere of a few minutes ago had disappeared. People's faces seemed softer and more human.

As I started to eat, I felt someone sit down next to me. I turned to look at them. It was The Taxi Driver. He had a newly grown stubbly beard and a shaved head. I didn't know if he was trying out a disguise or he'd couldn't be bothered grooming.

"How are you? I was worried about you. " I said. " I didn't know what had happened to you. I wasn't even sure if someone had tried to bump you off."

I hugged him hard and it seemed to take him a back though he didn't seem bothered by it.

"Who would bump me off?" He asked and roared with laughter.

"I wasn't sure. Stella, if she'd got hold of surveillance photos showing us in the ambulance or even Nico for drawing unwanted attention to The UR." I said.

The Taxi Driver roared with laughter for a second time. I didn't know what was so funny. He wiped the tears from his eyes.

"I don't get it." I said looking puzzled.

The Taxi Driver put his arm round me.

"Nico wouldn't dare bump me off, she'd get a thick ear. Imagine bumping off her dear old dad." He said.

My jaw dropped. I hadn't realized Nico was his daughter. That explained a lot. Both her sister and her husband had been killed by Nemo and co, that could harden anyone's heart.

"So, Nico and Jane were sisters?" I said "Do you have any other kids?" I asked.

"One more daughter but she was adopted years ago. I think I know where she is but just going to give it some time before letting her know that I'm her dad. She might not want to know. That's always the risk when you've had to give someone up." He said, sadly.

I just nodded quietly.

"Do you ever have any doubts about all of this?" I asked.

"You were sat next to me in that ambulance, weren't you?" He said " I am always weighing stuff up. I don't ever want people to be injured, let alone die. That's the whole point to avoid that. But as you said yourself the other day, we were being shot at, what do you do? "He looked at me right in the eye.

"When I was in the office the other day and that guy died. Was he really ok with that? I think maybe some people see themselves as soldiers for a cause but I don't and I don't want to be a martyr even if Nico thinks I should be. "I said.

"I don't think you should worry about that. There are only a few specific people who will possibly be doing that and only those who are absolutely prepared to do it. It might not even be necessary. "He said.

"What are you two talking about? You look as thick as thieves." Nico appeared.

"Your dad was just reassuring me. "I said. I was glad to know that The Taxi Driver was ok and also that he seemed to be a bit of a steadying influence on Nico, at least I hoped he was.

"Yes, he's good at that, aren't you Dad?" She said and gave a slightly strange smile that I couldn't quite read. He looked at me right in the eyes.

"You mustn't take too much notice of Nico. Her heart is in the right place and whatever she does is for the right reason, babe ok? Whatever happens don't forget that ok?"

It felt like a warning. I was sure that the Taxi Driver knew more about what was about to happen than he was letting on. I looked at him and couldn't help but feel really sad. Everything was uncertain and I was a stranger in an unfamiliar place. Tomorrow seemed too soon in coming and I dreaded what I would wake up to in the morning.

****

CHAPTER 27

I was alone in my bunk. No one was billeted with me in the end. I hadn't seen Ellen or her nurse or doctor. I hoped they'd been evacuated with all of the other members of The UR. I didn't want to think about what would happen if they hadn't. I hadn't plucked up the courage to read what was written in the manifesto, it frightened me. The whole idea of it set me on edge. So, with trepidation, I took it out from inside my bag and laid it out on the bunk bed.

I opened the first page. It read:

This is the manifesto of " The Underground Resistance." Our reason for being is to disrupt, dismantle and destroy those agents who would wish to interfere with the democratic rights of the ordinary person. There are many individuals, companies and organizations who would try to prevent individuals from exercising their ability to vote, to work with representation or the right to safety.

There are many ways we will do this. We will always attempt to do this peacefully but if needed, will use any means necessary to achieve our ends. We will not tolerate attacks on the people by any corporation or individual. If we become aware of any plans by anybody or group to cause harm to the people, either as a whole or individuals. We will shut them down either by mounting a serious DDOS attack or by causing physical disruption to either work or domestic premises. We will ensure that each and every target is no longer operational. We will cause reputational damage that will be very difficult to quell."

I stopped reading for a moment. The UR certainly wanted to

fight fire with fire. I was feeling very much in two minds. So far, I hadn't read anything too extreme other than using any means necessary but that in itself was something I didn't feel entirely comfortable with.

I continued on reading wondering what my role would be.

"We are entirely committed to the destruction of any organization or individual who wish to carry out testing, authorized or unauthorized on individuals or groups of the people as a whole. We will do this by any means necessary.

Be completely aware, if you are involved in any of the organizations, corporations or governments who sanction the use of these tests upon the population will be regarded as an enemy of The Underground Resistance. Consider this to be a declaration of war. If you think you are able to hide from us be aware, wherever you are we will find you."

I lay back on my bunk and breathed a large sigh. I didn't like the way the manifesto seemed to be authorizing violence on a large scale. It also threw open a lot of questions. If you were a member of a government who had secretly authorised tests but you hadn't known about personally, were you culpable or a legitimate target. If you found yourself disgraced or worse, could it be justified? I wasn't sure it could be. There are sometimes good people involved in bad governments.

If you are a member of a company who took contracts to test but worked in an office and never was involved in the planning or didn't see the secret plans and would never have access to them, were they a legitimate target? I didn't think so. I thought they might have been as appalled by these contracts as we were.

I heard people being called to the central hall throughout the evening. I couldn't help wondering what they were being asked to do. Declarations of war need foot soldiers to carry out the battles. I hoped that all of them would be able to walk away from the next few days relatively unscathed. I hoped that I would be able to too.

****

After what seemed like a few hours, the lights turned off automatically and the speakers went silent. I found myself, growing drowsy. I still had no idea what I was expected to do. Part of me didn't want to know. I felt very apprehensive for the day ahead. I felt a bit like I was in a prison cell but without the view from the window. It was entirely claustrophobic and the walls were so thick that no sounds could squeak through. It was utterly black and silent.

There was no distraction at all from my thoughts and they circled round and round within my head. They seemed to be getting louder and louder. I realized that I had surrendered control to a large extent. Without a clock, it meant that time had disappeared unless I checked my phone. I was thankful that the doors weren't locked because not being able to see or hear was difficult enough. I couldn't help feeling that maybe the members of The UR themselves were being tested. How many of us could cope without being able to be in command of our own lighting or being able to take in a view from outside of the window? Was there those for whom the silence was so all encompassing that they could be encouraged to do anything, if only someone would turn the sound up again. There are no bigger bullies than those that reside inside your mind, a wise man once said. Those bullies never become louder than in the darkness and silence. They can tear a vulnerable mind to pieces and so there is a reason that sensory deprivation is used to wear people down through torture.

I was glad of my phone. It could keep things clear in my mind by telling me the date and time but I also was truly grateful for the small light that cut through the darkness and silence. I knew however, that the battery wasn't infinite and I hadn't noticed anywhere obvious to charge it. It was important to ration it because I had no idea how long we would be here or indeed what would happen next.

J.E. CLARKSON

****

CHAPTER 28

Voices started to come through the speakers in different languages. It was confusing and disconcerting. A purple light shone in under the door and a low rumble unfurled around the bunker. I went to the door and found it open. I expected to see other people at their door ways but there was no one there except for me.

The voices continued and I looked in the opened bedrooms. There was no one to be seen. I felt the rumbling becoming more vigorous under the floor, until it knocked me off my feet. Then it stopped, just like that. The entire corridor and all of the dormitories were bathed in purple light. I picked myself up and carried on walking. Intermittently, I saw clouds of dust float down from the ceiling through the vents. As the dust floated down, the light picked it up and as it fell it seemed to sparkle purple. It was surreal walking through clouds of shimmering purple with the only sound being various voices speaking languages that I didn't understand.

I kept on walking hoping to run into someone, anyone so that I could ask them what had happened. I reached the central hall and found it to be completely empty like everywhere else. The Underground Resistance logo was still forming a backdrop to the stage but it had been ripped in half. The podium had also been knocked over and the microphones and their wires sprawled across the stage like spiders' legs. I looked across at the chairs and tables that had been so neatly arranged into rows earlier and saw that they'd been overturned and strewn across the room just as though they'd been thrown around in a fit of rage.

I had a terrible feeling that something ominous had happened maybe it was the population testing experiment outlined in the Nemo and Co. secret file? Had the Underground been wiped out or had they evacuated? But if so, why had they left me here alone. Suddenly the foreign language voices stopped broadcasting. Simultaneously the purple lights changed colour to white and a very tall chrome figure appeared from behind the remaining cloth behind the stage. It was Stella. She was holding what appeared to be a detonator in her right hand.

At first, she said nothing and we both just stared at each other, just the two of us, alone in the chaos.

"What are you doing here?" I eventually asked.

"I don't know why you ask." She said "You know what my job is. I know you know."

I shivered slightly. The clinical way in which Stella spoke of mass destruction

and murder was completely chilling. I couldn't understand why I hadn't been disturbed. I also couldn't understand where everyone had gone. They had disappeared without a trace as if they had never even existed.

"There's something very important that you don't know. That no one has told you yet." She said.

"What do you mean?" I said.

She walked around me in a circle looking me up and down. I felt like I was being sized up by a big cat stalking its next kill.

"You were adopted, weren't you? You were given up as a baby and left in a children's home. You never knew who your parents were as they gave you up as soon as you were born." Stella said.

"What's that got to do with anything? I was well looked after when I left the home. My adoptive Mum and Dad were my real Mum and Dad when they were still alive. No one could've looked after me better." I said.

Stella continued to walk around me making a slight whirring sound as she walked. Her feet clanked against the wooden floor and scraped slightly as she moved slightly more slowly.

"Did you ever wonder if you had other brothers or sisters when you were growing up? Other than those who lived with your adoptive parents?" Stella said.

"No. Yes .... well sometimes, I suppose but I still don't understand what that has to do with why you're here?" I said.

"Have you noticed any family resemblances while you've been here. Anyone where you look at their faces and think that it's just like looking into a mirror?" Stella said.

I was puzzled. I hadn't noticed any one who I thought looked like me. I'd never considered my birth parents much. I didn't blame them and hadn't really wanted to be reconciled with them either, they'd just been a chapter of

my life that had been closed for a long time and so not really even thought about.

"Oh, come on." Stella said. " You can't be so unobservant. Think hard. I'm not going to make this too easy for you, especially when it's so obvious."

I hadn't really talked to anyone while I'd been here other than......and then it dawned on me.

"Are you saying that The Taxi Driver is my Dad and Nico is my sister?" I said.

"You got there in the end." Stella said. " Why did you think they were so intent in recruiting you? Apart from the fact that you worked for us, of course."

"How long have you known?" I said.

"I've always known." Stella said. " It's my job. Information remember, and that's why I recruited you. They were desperate to find you and after I saw your online CV and knew of your financial problems, I knew that it would be an easy way to hook you in. That was the first part of the plan and it worked didn't it?"

"So, what's the second part?" I asked.

"Well, this is why I'm here." She said and suddenly stopped walking.

She looked straight at me and then I noticed she pressed a button on the detonator. Then everything went black.

****

CHAPTER 29

Day?

Was I alive or was I dead? I didn't know. I couldn't see anything at all but I could hear a constant beep and I could feel a sharp pain in my arm. I felt around a bit with my hands. I realized that I couldn't move my legs or back at all but my arms could move freely. I was obviously alive but where I was, I didn't know.

"She's coming around." Said a voice that I didn't recognize.

"Yes, it was touch and go there for a little bit but she's a fighter." Said another voice that I didn't recognize.

I decided to stay silent to see if I could glean any information that they would be less likely to share if they could see that I was compus mentus.

"She was talking about some robot. I don't know where she got that from. Maybe the sedative and opioid dose is a bit high. Let's just reduce it slightly to see if it makes any difference."

Were they saying that I was imagining Stella? How had I got here in the first place if not because of Stella. I saw her with the detonator in her hand. I was sure of it.

Light began to gradually filter through to my eyes. I could see a blur of colours at first and shapes that I couldn't make sense of. But gradually, things came back into focus. I began to become aware that my eyes must have been bandaged. I began to blink as the light was difficult to adjust to. It was so bright that it made my eyes hurt.

"Just take it steady. You've been very lucky. You nearly died." The first voice I didn't recognize spoke.

I looked at them. They were wearing a mask and hazmat suit. They were obviously either a nurse or doctor. I also realized that the constant beeping was a heart monitor.

"Where am I?" I asked.

"You're in the hospital. You've been caught up in an explosion. You were found alone in a disused Cold War bunker. They don't really know why you were there. We're also running some tests because you seem to have picked up a strange virus and we don't know where from." The second voice spoke.

It was a lot to take in but this was obviously what the secret USB file was referring to. I was still confused about where the other members of The Underground Resistance were. I didn't think it was wise to mention Stella as they obviously thought that I was labouring under some sort of delusion as it was.

"How long have I been here?" I asked.

"About a month. You seem to have recovered now from the virus but we're really unsure of how infectious you are? So hence the hazmat suits. You've been in a medically induced coma for most of that time to give your body a chance to fight the virus and recover." The second voice said.

"Was anybody else affected?" I asked.

"Not where you were but there have been one or two people affected by strange symptoms throughout the city. We're just keeping an eye on it." The first voice said.

"Have I had any visitors at all? I asked

" I'm afraid that you haven't and aren't allowed any until we can work out whether you're still infectious or not. But maybe we can review that once we've found out. Did you have anyone particular in mind?" The first voice asked.

"A couple of people." I said "but I don't know where they are. I thought they were in the bunker at the time of the explosion like I was but you said that there was no one else there so I don't know where they could be."

"Just try to get some more rest and we can try to work all of that out once we've confirmed you're not infectious." The second voice said.

Both of the figures looked at each other, picked up my notes and then walked out of the room.

I looked around me to take in the hospital room. I appeared to be in some kind of plastic bubble. I wasn't hooked up to any oxygen just the heart monitor. I was attached to a drip which was pumping in both liquid and drugs, I guessed. There were no plants in the room and it was completely white from the tiles on the floor, to the walls and ceiling. I also noticed that there were no windows to the outside world. I could be anywhere at all and was none the wiser. I did notice though that there was a window where the medical staff could keep an eye on me. It reminded me more of the mirrored window found in a police interrogation room than in any hospital room that I had ever seen.

I could not see who was in there observing me. I hoped, there was only the medical staff but in spite of their feeling that I was in some kind of drugged stupor that was causing me to hallucinate, I was fairly sure that I hadn't imagined either Stella or The Underground Resistance though I could see that to someone unfamiliar with either of them, it would seem at least a bit farfetched.

I was very concerned about what had happened to The Taxi Driver, Ellen, Janey and even to some extent Nico. They seemed to have disappeared without a trace. I wondered if they might have been some of the other virus cases and were being holed up in another bubble in this or some other unknown hospital.

I felt that it was a question that I couldn't ask the medical staff. Maybe they didn't know anyway. I looked at the mirrored window trying to fathom things out but the strange thing was that in spite of the mirror, I could have sworn that I saw a very tall chrome figure stood there looking right back at me.

****

CHAPTER 30

Day?

For a long time, how long I didn't know, I seemed to inhabit a netherworld between sleeping and wakefulness but I didn't really know which was which. From time to time, I saw the hazmat suited figures moving around the bed adjusting dosages bringing food and drink and making notes. They very rarely said anything to me and I didn't ask them much because I didn't think they'd tell me anything if I did.

I didn't really feel in any pain and couldn't remember much about any symptoms of the virus but then I had been asleep for a month and so must have slept through the majority.

Sometimes, I could've sworn that people I knew had visited on the other side of the plastic bubble. One time it seemed that Ellen had stood over the bed reading my favourite book to me and begging me to pull through. Even though she was wearing a mask I was fairly sure it was her. Even with most of her face covered I recognized her somehow. I knew that that must've been a dream as she couldn't have found her way to wherever I was, being hooked up to machinery herself. I also thought her hair was bright, fuchsia pink instead of its usual copper.

Then there was the time that The Taxi Driver and Janey seemed to bring my food in and talk to me about rehab. I was vaguely aware of them and tried to mention something about The Underground Resistance but they just appeared slightly confused. I thought it was better to not mention too much more with The UR being a secret organization. Everything just seemed so scrambled up in my brain but yet I didn't feel any-thing much. I wasn't really angry, happy or sad. I just felt like I was in a big cloud or marshmallow, floating above everyone and everything. I wasn't even that curious.

It was funny how everyone and everything seemed like it was under water. Even the sound of people talking was like it came from the bottom of a swimming pool. I wondered how I would adjust back to a kind of normal life as none of this was normal in any way. I didn't think I had a job now seeing as Stella seemed to have been responsible for the explosion that had put me in here. I felt fairly relaxed about that. Maybe it was the pain killers or maybe the drama before I was hospitalised had left me with a desire for a less dramatic occupation. Either way I wasn't in a great rush to get back to any sort of work, let alone spying.

****

Recovery seemed to take forever and then it happened all at once. The plastic bubble was removed and I was moved to a private room where masked medical staff attended to me and after a few days encouraged me to get up and start walking around.

I noticed there was no TV or Radio so no news or entertainment of any kind. I'd gone from one kind of bubble to another. One where the real world never intruded. Once I had moved to this new ward, I didn't have the feeling that any familiar faces were looking after me or coming to visit. So maybe they were drug fueled hallucinations or symptoms of the virus. But I had no way of knowing.

I missed the familiar and there were no windows to the outside world so my white, clinical environment was all there was. I imagined from time to time that this was what heaven was like. But I was pretty sure that I wasn't dead. As it was, one day just merged into the next.

****

CHAPTER 31

Day?

I began to feel that I may live the rest of my life in the hospital bed, unable to smell a flower or walk on a beach but then one of the doctors arrived with a wheelchair.

"Do you want to go to the garden?" They asked.

"There's a garden here?" I asked "

"Of a sort?" They said.

"Ok then. I'm getting a bit fed up of being in here." I said.

I gingerly got into the wheelchair and the doctor started pushing me out of the room. We walked into an all-white corridor. There were no windows and the strip lights in the ceiling were also very bright. The floor tiles were also a brilliant white.

"Not a lot of colour around here is there?" I said.

"I've never really noticed." The doctor said.

I found it very strange. To not notice the unnatural whiteness that was a characteristic of the hospital just seemed odd. I hadn't spent much time in hospital before now but any one that I had visited, let alone stayed in, was decorated in a mixture of colours. I had never seen a place like it.

It probably took us ten minutes to get to the door to the garden. We saw no other medical staff, porters or patients. There was only myself and the doctor. I wondered if I was the only patient in the entire hospital. I didn't even notice any other doors to other wards. I tried to shake off the unsettling thought that this was yet another installment in the weird story that my life had recently become.

The doctor pushed the doors open and I couldn't believe what I saw. This was not a usual garden by any measure. There were benches and approximations of plants and trees but they weren't living, they were models. Ten feet tall trees with fabric leaves and what looked like polystyrene bark. There was even a fake, stuffed bird perched on one of the branches. I looked at the horizon and it seemed to be a printed backdrop like one of those you'd find in a faded old bar.

"What is this place?" I asked " This isn't like any garden I've ever seen? What the hell is going on?"

"Try not to get too upset. It's very important that you try to keep calm in order to help your recovery." The doctor said.

"How can I keep calm? This is the weirdest place, I've ever seen. It's all white, there's no other patients and the garden is made from fake plants and what looks like a dodgy poster." I said." What's worse is that you don't find it weird at all."

"I don't know any different. I've worked here for years. It's all done to keep the patient safe." The doctor said.

"Safe from what?" I asked.

"When you're a patient here there's usually someone or some-thing who means you harm." The doctor replied. "So, we need to protect you and keep you inside. That's why the garden is as it is."

I felt totally claustrophobic but more than that I was furiously angry. This surely had something to do with either The UR or Nemo and Co. yet again. When would my life return to normal again and when would I stop being a pawn between them?

"Whoever your boss is, I want to see them." I said.

"I don't know what you mean." Said the doctor.

"You know exactly what I mean." I said " If I'm being kept here, I want to know why and by whom."

"But I'm not supposed to leave you alone." They said.

"I don't care. If you don't fetch them, I am going to take off and considering I can't walk and don't know where I am, that could end up with me getting hurt or lost and you getting in trouble with your boss, which I'm guessing will be bad news for you and being in this thing I've got a natural advantage so please go and get them."

The doctor realized that I was serious but also, I sensed that I'd hit the nail on the head as far as whoever the boss was. The doctor seemed extremely nervous all of a sudden.

"There's no need for all of that." The doctor said. " I'll see what I can do but I can't promise anything. They're very busy."

With that they left me in my wheelchair and disappeared through the hospital doors. I sat and just looked around. I wondered how many other patients had been brought here and sat in this bizarre place. Not in any universe did this look like a garden. It made me think that any person resident here was either so far gone on painkillers that they didn't notice or they were so utterly brainwashed that they were unable to question it.

"So, we meet again." A familiar metallic voice greeted me with an almost weary sigh.

"Stella." I said. " What a surprise."

She walked towards me slightly jerkily. I looked at her hands to see if she was carrying any weaponry in her hands like the last time we met. Thankfully her hands were empty, but it didn't mean that I trusted her any more for it.

"Why do you insist on being so difficult?" She said. " We're only trying to look after you."

I laughed and laughed for a few minutes. Then shook my head.

"Oh yes. Really trying to look after me, by blowing me up the last time we met. I'm wondering what on earth my care involves here. Being drugged up to the eyeballs with God knows what! Even being infected with a virus. Brilliant care here. No wonder there's anyone else here apart from me. " I said.

I wondered if anyone had actually survived their stay here. I was determined that I would, even if it was primarily to frustrate Stella. If it was even possible to annoy an android.

"I didn't blow you up. I merely removed you from one dimension to another." Stella said.

"What does that even mean?" I said.

"It was necessary to make sure that yourself and The Underground Resistance were separated. With you removed and the termination of their other agent, The Underground Resistance don't have any inside agents in the company now. That's just how we want it. They have been getting too close. We have to ensure that the plans we have been tasked to carry out actually happen. So, we have an emergency plan that we sometimes need to use to make sure that other people don't get in the way." Stella said.

I looked at her and she seemed to grow larger and more menacing with every moment.

"So, you've removed me to here. Wherever here is." I said.

"Yes. To all your resistance friends, they will just think that you've vanished. They will be looking around at the surrounding hospitals and mortuaries to see if you're being cared for or if your body shows up. But of course, you won't because you're here."

"They'll find me eventually if they're checking hospitals." I said.

"They won't find this one and they'll be looking forever for it. I told you, you've moved dimensions. To The Resistance, this dimension doesn't even exist. The hospital and all of the doctors and nurses don't exist and have never existed. If I placed you back into your usual life and you told anyone, even your best friends, no one would believe you. You're effectively in a time capsule and I can keep you here as long as I want. I promise you that you will be well looked after and well fed. I will even sort out a tv for you so that you have entertainment. But you are staying here at least until the tests are complete. " Stella said.

The blood drained from my face. It was one of the most sinister things I'd ever heard of. That Nemo and Co. could ensure that their rivals were disappeared, meant that it would be almost impossible to keep them held to account by anyone. I didn't exist in my actual life anymore. I had been removed to my own limbo. To a purgatory that no one else knew existed. Or even knew was possible.

****

CHAPTER 32

I was totally alone. I knew that now, with only a metal psychopath and their minions for company. I had no idea how I would be able to get out of this situation. I hadn't been blown up. I had been disappeared and somehow infected with a virus. I had no idea how long I was to be kept in this form of isolation away from any other human beings. I sensed knowing Stella now as I did, that there was an element of torture in my being kept here.

I sensed that the medical staff were trying to keep me off balance emotionally and mentally. I even wondered now if some of the conversations that I'd overheard when I was in my bed had been staged, whether they actually realized that I was in fact conscious at the time. I didn't suppose that I'd ever know.

I was determined to be as mentally sharp as possible so this meant refusing to take any of the oral drugs. I had to do this and dispose of them secretly. Anything put through the drip would be more difficult. I also had to see whether any of the staff might be open to helping me out or if they were all entirely loyal to Stella and Nemo and Co. It was a seemingly Herculean task. I didn't have any idea how I would be able to escape from Stella's isolation unit. But nonetheless, I would try.

****

I concluded that my plan had to be constructed and carried out totally in my head to begin with. I knew that Stella would ensure that there would be almost total surveillance within the walls of the hospital so my first task would be to find out where all of the cameras were. Then change my behaviour accordingly.

None of the cameras were obvious ones. I sat in my bed and

looked around the room and tried to look at the points where cameras could be. I was fairly sure that there could be one concealed in the ceiling light. So, when the nurse appeared with my tablets in the morning and evening, I made sure to keep the tablets in my mouth and pretend to eat them whilst the nurse was still in the room. Then once they'd left the room I hid under the covers and spat the pills out and stored them under the pillow. I soon had quite a few. I wasn't a hundred percent sure that I'd avoided the camera but if I hadn't, no one had confronted me about it.

I also knew that once the lights went out that I could make plans and even test out how closely I was being watched by my keepers. I wasn't able to move very far as I was still hooked up to machinery and a drip but I did figure out that it would be possible for me to manoeuvre myself around the bed without unhooking the drip or getting caught up in it. I realized again after a couple of evenings doing this, that they either did not have night vision cameras or if they did, they were biding their time before they took me to task or at least asked me what I was doing.

Once I'd stopped talking the pills, I did notice a subtle change. I still felt foggy headed so was fairly sure that something was being fed into me intravenously but still there was a difference. I also decided to ask to be taken into the garden as much as possible, mainly so that I could scope out the building as much as I could. I wanted to memorise the outlay till I knew it like the back of my hand. I noticed as we made our way down the corridor that there were five doors on the left-hand side and five on the right. I noticed that the second door on the left had a sign on it reading, Strictly no entry: authorised staff only.

The door was always closed but I noticed that at times there was a strange light emanating from under it. It was rather like the purple light I remembered seeing when I was in the corridor of the bunker. I resolved that somehow, I needed to get in there. There was obviously some link with what had happened in the bunker and what was happening inside that room. I knew that the two nurses who wheeled me out to the garden were unlikely to be a great deal of help to me. They almost seemed to have been drugged themselves as they had very little to say about anything. They also seemed to avoid eye contact. They just seemed like pallid facsimiles of real people.

I wondered if it would be possible to get to know either of them more closely, even to enlist them to my cause. I had a feeling that they had been disappeared themselves.

I suddenly became very curious about them. If they'd also been transported here because they had posed a threat to Nemo and Co's plans, they might be more amenable to rebelling against Stella but being able to find out what they had done and why they had been sent here, I sensed would be extremely difficult.

****

.E. CLARKSON

Day?

One morning I woke up and I saw that a TV had been bolted to the wall. I hadn't been aware of when it had been brought in. It must have been while I was asleep which was extremely unsettling. I hadn't heard a thing and yet at the same time, I was glad of the distraction. Or at least I thought I would be.

Suddenly it flashed on.

"Police and the authorities are looking for a city woman who has disappeared and has been connected to the murder of the hospital security guard who was hit by a stolen ambulance." The newsreader said.

I blinked in incredulity as my own photo appeared on the screen. It was a mocked-up mug shot.

"The suspect is well known to the authorities and is known to have been involved in a number of incidents in accordance with seditious elements trying to overthrow the government."

"You absolute bastards." I mouthed.

So, this was what was going to happen. I had become a piece of information that had been vanished, erased and changed in order to keep Stella's plans active. I wasn't sure if this was actually being shown on the news networks at home or if this had been mocked up specially to try and keep me in my box.

I knew very little other than I was not going to react. They were banking on that and I wasn't prepared to give them the satisfaction. I realized more than ever that I had to stay mentally strong and independent of the influence of Stella's propaganda as far as possible.

"We are currently unaware of the suspect's name so if you have any information that can aid our enquiries please call the number at the bottom of the screen. "The newsreader said.

I sat in bed fuming. I felt like throwing things around the room but once again was determined not to. At that moment, the nurse arrived with my breakfast.

"How do you like your new TV?" They asked.

I wasn't going to rise to it. I wasn't even sure that they were in on any scheme that Stella might have.

"Yes, it's ok. Nice surprise to have it there when I woke up. I don't know how you were able to fit it when I was asleep, very skillful." I said.

They looked slightly startled.

"Well, we wanted to make sure that you got a proper rest. It's very important for your recovery. You need to sleep as much as possible and stay really calm. Now eat your breakfast and I will bring around your tablets for you."

The nurse left. I was none the wiser as to whether they knew about what was going on or whether they were in on it. They seemed completely blank and unaware almost more of an automaton than Stella. Still, I didn't completely trust them either. It could all be part of an act. So, I prepared to dispose of the pills as usual.

Another programme flashed up on the TV screen. This time it wasn't a news programme, but a documentary on The Underground Resistance. It painted a portrait of a band of violent criminals who wanted to do no nothing more than harm upstanding people and cause chaos around the city and the country as a whole. It wasn't very subtle. I wanted to shout out for Stella to hear.

"Stop treating me like a complete idiot."

But of course, I didn't. I wondered what would happen next. Constant heavy metal played loudly throughout the night? I was beginning to think that she wasn't as clever as she thought she was. I gained some hope then, because I knew that I wasn't the cleverest person in the world but I knew the importance of my own mind. And because I knew what she did and how she used information to manipulate people, I had some defence against what she was trying to do.

I began to feel defiant about it. If I was staying in a different dimension then any made up information about me at home couldn't do much damage when I wasn't there. I couldn't be arrested for the moment and if it was all made up for my benefit, then it wasn't working anyway. I made a decision at that point that I was going to try to record what was happening to me whilst I was here, mentally at first and then make some written or visual record. Then I had to find somewhere safe to store it all. Somewhere where Stella and her all seeing eyes wouldn't be able to find it. The question was where?

****

CHAPTER 33

The Stella Broadcasting Corporation continued its programming constantly over the next day. The programmes covered a number of different subjects. All of them either saying how wonderful Nemo and Co were and how terrible The Underground Resistance were. It was almost comical. My personal favourite was a kid's programme where the owner of Nemo and Co, Mr. Nemo appeared and hired trainees were installed in key positions inside the company. Seeing the owner, a thin balding man who seemed to have a permanent sneer on his face, trying to suppress his obvious nastiness, in order to come across as a magnanimous master of finance, as he condescended to a group of teenagers that he seemed to believe were way beneath him.

The teenagers of course ran rings around him and in the end seemed to run his company better than he did. I constantly thought, can't he see himself and how silly he looks? But then I thought that he probably suffered from the same character flaw that so many powerful people often do that they think that because they are good at one thing, that they are good at everything. Sadly, it seemed to me that the only thing that he seemed to be really good at was sneering.

No wonder he needs Stella, I thought. He seemed like a little boy playing at a villain, a cardboard baddy who needed to puff himself up in order to intimidate others. But he just wasn't very charismatic or scary on his own. The only thing that was legitimately frightening was that such a man had so much power when he was so unsuitable in being able to wield it.

The second program that featured Mr. Nemo was trying to play up his machismo and ability to bully people into doing what he wanted. All of the employees featured seemed to spend their time bowing and scraping to a terribly spoiled baby. I was willing one of them to pour cold tea on his head or tell him to bugger off. Sadly, none of them did but I realised that I did recognise one of those employees and when I realised who they were it gave me a shiver of delight. It was one of the nurses and seeing how Mr. Nemo had humiliated them, I was fairly certain that given the right opportunity, I might be able to talk them into helping me.

****

I must've nodded off without realising. There was a very strange alarm blaring away, not loudly but yet it seemed to vibrate right through you. The strange purple light appeared again and I found that I was no longer hooked up to the drip any more. The TV was still screwed to the wall but the only thing that was playing was interference.

I looked under the pillow to see if the pills were still there. They weren't but it was like they never had been as the sticky residue was no longer there either. I found I could leave the bed and thought I would attempt to leave the room. It was worth the risk as no one appeared to be anywhere close by. The usual sounds of the medical staff walking up and down wheeling trolleys or wheel chairs were completely absent. There was only the vibration of the quiet alarm and the eerie purple light to keep me company.

On the floor outside the door of my room, I found my burner phone.

"How did you get here?" I said and bent down to pick it up. I dropped it again almost straightaway as it was so hot it burned. I looked around to see if there was anything that I could use to pick it up. I realised if I took the pillowcase from the bed that I could fold it up and place it into the pocket of my dressing gown. I quickly ran into the bedroom and grabbed the pillowcase, fearful that if I took too long that the phone might have disappeared again by the time, I made it outside the door again. Thankfully, it was still there so I picked it up with the pillow-case and put it in my pocket.

As I got up, I thought I noticed a nurse pushing another patient towards the garden in a wheelchair. I flattened myself against the wall and rapidly looked up to the ceiling to see if there were any plausible places for cameras. The only likely places seemed like the light fittings again. I waited for a few seconds to see if any other medical staff would appear to make me go back to bed but they didn't. I reached inside my pocket to see if the phone had cooled down. It was still warm but was now just cool enough for me to handle it without needing the pillowcase.

"You're not the only one who can make videos Stella". I thought. Then I started filming.

I began by making my way down the corridor, filming all of the doors and especially the door that featured the Strictly no entry, sign. I didn't feel confident enough to try to get into the room but it did seem as though the purple light that covered everything seemed to be filtering out from there. And yet, as I continued to film, I noticed that the door was opened just a crack. I resolved that it was worth the risk trying to get in to film what was in there even if it became dangerous. So, I very carefully, manoeuvered myself through the gap in the door way and went in.

****

CHAPTER 34

I fully expected to be caught almost straight away, given a good telling off and hauled back to bed by the scruff of the neck. But it didn't happen, so very carefully, I continued to film and moved slowly forward.

There appeared to be a number of television screens at the back of the room which seemed far longer and wider than it had from the outside. In front of the screens were a desk which appeared to be a desk for the controlling of whatever happened in this room.

Then between me and the TV screens there was a large table, big enough to hold a human being on it. I noticed some sinister bindings that looked like arm and leg, even neck cuffs. It was obviously there as a kind of torture device or at the very least to hold a person in place. It made me feel sick. I knew well enough not to trust Stella, but there was something about this that just made the other things seem even worse. That she could stand there and lie so smoothly and almost elegantly about wanting to take care of people when they were patently doing the opposite was shocking to witness, even though in my heart of hearts, I already knew it was the case.

From behind I heard the sound of the door opening more widely. I was grateful that it creaked a little bit because it gave me just enough time to hide in one of the dark corners of the room.

It was one of the nurses, I was pretty sure she was the same one who'd been wheeling around the other patient towards the gardens earlier. I tried to breathe as quietly as possible. I felt like each breath was louder than a bugle call but thankfully I wasn't discovered. I still had a decent viewpoint to be able to document what was happening.

The TV screens turned on, half of them appeared to show Mr. Nemo and half of them showed Stella. It was like a jigsaw puzzle with each of the pieces fitting together to form each face.

"Did you manage to transfer them over?" Mr. Nemo said.

"Yes." The Nurse answered.

"I know that it's highly unusual for you to take two patients in at once but we think that the other girl might just help quell her rebellion." Mr. Nemo said.

"Well, we're just here to carry out the plans that you've made." The nurse said.

"Excellent, Excellent. I will leave you with Stella and she'll work out all of the details with you. And remember that the sooner you sort this out, the more quickly we'll arrange for you to see your husband again. Maybe your daughter too if you're really lucky."

With that Mr. Nemo's image disappeared from the screens. So that's how he controls them. I was appalled but not so surprised. It was the same as with Stella. Intimidate people. Scare them into doing what you want. I hoped that the Nurse was able to rebel but that's incredibly difficult when threats to your family are being used against you. Keeping you from your children was particularly low, I thought.

"So, you have put the other patient into room two, is that correct?" Stella said.

"Yes." The nurse said.

"That's great, it's not too close to enable them to fraternise too much and start hatching plans but it is near enough for her to be seen and for us to use her when necessary. Get her settled in and then we'll send you some more instructions." Stella said and then her face disappeared.

Once the screen went black, the nurse stuck two fingers up at it.

I was glad to witness it. The nurse was obviously being coerced into action and I was glad to see her rebelling against it even if she couldn't do it openly. I began to think that maybe it could be possible to ensure that Mr. Nemo and Stella wouldn't have everything their own way, even in here. I was curious though also as to who the other patient was? They obviously wanted to use them to get to me. I'd understood that much at least. I supposed it wouldn't be long until I met them again but more likely face to face and in some kind of engineered fashion but at least I knew about it. Forewarned is forearmed.

****

CHAPTER 35

Sneaking back into my bedroom wasn't easy. I kept having to find dark nooks which are difficult to find in the midst of a bright white corridor but somehow, I managed it. I was still amazed that I hadn't been caught yet. I found it weird, actually. It was almost just too easy and I was extremely suspicious about that. It was like I was being watched still to see what I would do. I could sense it somehow but I didn't know how or from where exactly. I thought the light fixtures most likely but even wondered if the camera phone or the TV hid a surveillance camera. Anything was possible in here. But if they did know, they weren't giving anything away. The silence was deafening.

Once I was sat back in my bed, I played back the footage that I'd filmed. It was pretty grainy but at least I'd managed to get something. I was looking forward to the day that I'd be able to confront Nemo and Stella with the footage. To be able to show the world how they truly were. It was a terrible secret to hold. I wished that it wasn't necessary. But their plan threatened so many anonymous people who didn't know it, who'd were going to be drawn into becoming Guinea Pigs without their consent. I was also furious that they had tried to make me disappear, that they had filled me full of drugs in order to render me helpless. They had considered me nothing but an impediment to their plans and as such felt that they had the right to upend my life to prevent me from interfering.

A quiet tap on the door interrupted my chain of thought. It was the nurse.

"Hello. I just wanted to let you know that another patient has joined us for the short term. As far as I'm aware, I think you may already know her, quite well in fact." She said.

I pretended to know nothing about it.

"Oh yes, who is it?" I asked.

"She's called Ellen, I believe. You knew her before, didn't you?" She said.

"Yes, she's my best friend. How is she doing? Is she conscious? Last time I saw her she was hooked up to a lot of machinery." I said.

Half of me was really excited that Ellen was here and there was the possibility that we could maybe spend some time together but the other half of me was really afraid for her. Knowing what I knew about what Nemo and Stella were capable of, made my blood run cold and I hated the idea that after what had already happened to her that she would have to go through any more suffering purely in order to control me.

"She is conscious. She's very confused and has been quite angry while she's been here but she is talking or should I say yelling. We've had to give her a little something to calm her down a bit just so she doesn't hurt herself. But I'm sure when she's had a good rest, she'll feel a bit better. Maybe you can go and have a chat with her in the garden tomorrow?" The nurse said.

"I'd love to if she's up to it. I don't want to tire her out." I said.

"Well, we'll see how it goes tomorrow." The nurse said and left.

I laid back wondering how they might try to use Ellen this time. Maybe it was another of their experiments to see how far you can push a person before they break. Or maybe it was a way to use one person's caring for another to nudge them into behaving in any way you wanted, like they had so ably demonstrated with the nurse, even though they didn't realise, maybe, that I knew about it.

The purple light disappeared and as it did, the TV flickered on again. I was unsurprised to see Stella's face appear on there.

"Welcome to our new patient we are very glad to have you with us. I hear you've had a little bit of trouble settling in. I think that I should let you know, that our hospital is founded upon the principles of behavioural science. So, if you behave well, you're rewarded and if you behave badly you will be punished. We have many ways in which we are able to do this. We know more about you than you do yourself. Just be aware of that." She said.

Poor Ellen, I thought. She doesn't know anything about Stella and Nemo, she has no idea that she's found herself resident in a psychopathic hospital ran by the experimenter in chief and his metal sidekick. I wished that I had never met them or answered the advert that I now knew had been planted there like a baited hook to see if I would take it. I like the eager fish being reeled in but what was worse so now was Ellen and she had never asked for it. She just happened to be my friend and got sucked into it.

"This can be a very comfortable place if you can work with us rather than against us and often, we find that those patients who are cooperative have shorter stays than those who work against us. We can also arrange visits from friends which can be really helpful as staying in hospital can be quite lonely at times." Stella continued.

I wondered why she had made me privy to what was being broadcast in Ellen's room. I was fairly sure that there was some hidden agenda behind it. Nothing was ever done without one.

"We have a lovely garden here for you to enjoy either by yourself or with a friend. So please consider everything I've said as friendly advice and then we'll get along just fine." Stella said and then her face disappeared from the screen.

I strained to see if I could hear anything from beyond the bounds of my own room. I thought I could hear distant shouting and screaming. Now and again, I did hear things crashing around. I decided to get out of bed and surreptitiously more into the door frame and eke out a slight gap, in order to try to view what was happening to Ellen down the corridor.

The crashing, screaming and banging around continued and I

heard the same, low vibration alarm as I had earlier. It hit you right in the chest. It wasn't a painful sensation but it was unsettling and I found myself becoming anxious. Whether it was caused by the alarm or it was down to concern for Ellen, I really didn't know. I managed to open the door very slightly without making a noise. I noticed that a number of medical staff ran down the corridor, I didn't know from where , wheeling a trolley into one of the bedrooms. It was similar to the trolley that I had seen from inside the secret operations room. It had restraining cuffs on it to keep an unruly patient in place. So, Stella had authorised Ellen's punishment. I was worried what form it might take and wanted to leave the room and come to her but I found myself rooted to the spot, unable to move even a single step further.

I was forced to watch as the medical staff wheeled Ellen, now restrained on the trolley towards the secret operations room. She screamed and yelled the entire way. As the entered the room, the low alarm stopped and the purple light appeared once again but this time it was brighter and seemed to fill all of the corners of the room it became so bright that I had to close my eyes but even then, it found its way in, seared onto my closed lids.

Then as suddenly as it started, the purple light disappeared again. The TV switched itself on once again this time showing corporate adverts for Nemo and Co. The first one featured their investments in drug companies and showed a generic family visiting a doctor who seemed straight from central casting, all shiny teeth and pristine white lab coat, who told them that all of their pain and suffering could be muted away by the regular ingestion of this new wonder drug, "Finax".

The next part of the advert showed said family engaging in a number of different activities including dancing, hand gliding and mountain climbing. The next advert featured a rehab clinic that was also bankrolled by Nemo and Co. They really have fingers in all of the pies, don't they? I thought. They're in charge of get you high and then in charge of trying to wean you off.

They're making money at both ends. I even wondered if this was another of their experiments. Making a population addicted to their drugs in order to make money and then creating a reason to get people off those drugs but because helping people to kick drugs is so notoriously difficult, keep sending people back to the Nemo and Co. rehab centre. Money pours in, people stay numbed and don't question anything. Opium is the new opium of the people and somewhere Marx is revolving in his grave.

I stopped watching the TV for a second and discovered that I could move my feet again somehow. The corridor was now silent and I realized that I could also hear the tiny squealing sound of wheels trundling towards me. Through the crack in the door, I could see that Ellen was being moved back into her room. She appeared to be sleeping but her head seemed to be lolling slightly to one side. It was a horrible sight. There were no other obvious signs of abuse but that didn't mean that there weren't any.

I tried to take in the full horror of what could be happening in the secret operations room. Something had been administered to her to stop her from protesting and I resolved to record it somehow the next time that it happened.

****

CHAPTER 36

Day?

We first met each other again a couple of days later, I think. I wasn't a hundred per cent sure as it was easy to lose track of time. I'd popped down to that strange garden to sit and have a look at the plastic trees. I didn't need a wheelchair anymore and the medical staff didn't seem to mind me wandering as long as they knew where I was.

I was fairly certain that the cameras were following me anyway so it wasn't as if I could go snooping without forward planning. I wasn't expecting to see Ellen. She just appeared wheeled in by one of the medical staff. I sat on a bench, hesitant not knowing whether to approach her or not. I didn't know if she would recognise me and didn't want to frighten her, but also because I didn't know whether the nurse would take kindly to it. I didn't want her to be punished for talking to me. She was suffering enough. In the end it was the nurse who suggested that I go and talk to her. She beckoned me over and I came and sat next to Ellen. It saddened me to see what she had become in such a short time of being resident here. She had lost weight and seemed like a shell of a person. Nothing like the shiny, full of life extrovert that I knew and loved. She just seemed to stare ahead unblinkingly, not taking anything in.

"Hi Ellen, it's me. "I said "Do you remember who I am?"

"Yes, my best friend." She said "I haven't seen you since the accident."

"What happened? I never got to the bottom of it. Last time I saw you, you were in a different hospital." I said, thinking that I had to be careful in what I said not wanting to give anything much away in case those who were watching us didn't know about it.

"I don't remember that." She said. "I can remember being on your settee. Some friend of yours that I didn't really know had arrived to pick me up from the interview. Some weird person had kept me waiting in a room ready to be called for the interview but I never was. They'd given me a cup of tea and quite soon after I started to feel quite ill. The next thing that I remember, there I was on your settee. I started to feel worse and worse and felt like I wanted to get some fresh air and then literally just as I got outside of your front door, someone pushed from behind and in front of a car. I don't remember much after that until I woke up here. And what a weird place it is. What's all that stuff on the TV all about and that robot? I don't understand any of it. Are we the only people here? I've not seen anyone else apart from the nurses and doctors." Ellen said.

"I think we're the only patients here because you're the first other person that I've seen since I came here. Why that is I don't really know." I said.

"Is this a psychiatric hospital?" Ellen asked. "I keep being taken off when I get angry, to somewhere, I don't know where. All I know is that I don't remember anything when I come back from there. I don't really feel anything either and it's slightly like my brain's been scrambled and it takes ages to become unscrambled again."

I wasn't sure what to say. I was confident that it was one of the many schemes and plans that Nemo and Stella would be using against us to try to grind us both down. In order to convince us that we were both mad and a way to wage psychological warfare against us. But I also just wondered whether this was another strand of experimentation to see how we would cope with the onslaught of various tactics.

"Who knows?" I said "All I know is that I was in one place and then I suddenly woke up and I was here."

"They keep telling me that I was suicidal." Said Ellen." But I wasn't. Not at all. I felt ill and gutted that I'd been pissed about with that interview but I didn't throw myself in front of the car. Someone pushed me. Every morning the nurse says it to me, but I know that it isn't true so I argue with them but they won't listen and then I get angry because they keep trying to tell me what I should think and feel. I know what I think and how I feel."

She sniffled slightly and I saw a tear flow across her cheek and drop onto the bench. I came and sat next to her.

"Of course, you do. No one can take that from you either, sometimes it's a good idea not to argue too hard with them. As long as you know what's going on in your head that's all that matters. Agree with them if it makes your life easier. No one can change what you think inside unless you let them." I said.

Ellen nodded quietly. She seemed to be taking everything in. I hoped that she would learn to choose her battles wisely because it seemed to me that Nemo and Stella were looking for any excuse to clamp down on any rebellion against them. They wanted to keep us in their iron grip like flies to be swatted away and done with as they willed it. They wanted total control I thought of anything and everything.

I wished I knew what had happened to Nico and The Taxi Driver. It didn't make much sense to me that they had just disappeared. I wondered if they had ended up being in patients here and then had been vanished again elsewhere. I had no way of knowing, but what I did know now, wary though I was about their methods, the alternative was far worse.

I had seen for myself, the depths that Nemo and co would sink to and not because I had read it in some document that someone else had shown me. I had experienced it myself in my own and Ellen's life, even in the apparent crushing dispersal of The Underground Resistance. I just kept coming back to the same thought. They will not accept any challenge at all. They will not allow resistance in any way. Anyone around them is expected to allow them. To behave with impunity whatever the consequences were. I couldn't go along with it.

The nurse appeared again to wheel Ellen away. I felt an intense sadness as she was wheeled away and all I could see was her shoulders slumping forwards and her head in her hands. I wondered how it must be for her, being transported to this truly weird place. To become aware that an entity such as Stella actually existed was enough to blow anyone's mind. No wonder that Ellen actually thought that she might be in a psychiatric hospital. I might've thought the same hadn't I been aware of all the secretive plans being concocted in the offices of Nemo and Co.

I wanted to talk to her about it so much. All about the bomb on the bus and the death of Cale Reed. I knew that she'd be appalled and disgusted. She'd want to be in on any sense of rebellion because of her complete sense of fairness. I wanted to talk to her about Nico Tucker, about Netty and the death of the security guard. I wanted to tell her about the facts being changed and manipulated in order to fit me up for something that I hadn't done. But if I hadn't lived through it myself, I would have had difficulty believing it. I wanted to tell her about being drugged and followed by Lawson and that she'd been right to deduce that he was one, very weird delivery man. I wanted to tell her that he'd followed her to the hospital and maybe tried to kill her and that Netty, someone that she didn't know and had never met had defended her from him and saved her life. But then I wasn't sure how she'd cope with knowing that he'd been killed in order to save her. It was enough of a burden for me.

I wondered how she would feel about knowing that a secret organisation had helped to smuggle her into their own private safe house in order to protect her, because she was my friend. But the thing that I had wanted to tell her the most was that I had found my biological Dad and sister. I'd almost forgotten about it since I'd woken up but somehow, I felt the pull of family stronger now than I had when The Taxi Driver first told me about it. I'd never felt like I missed my biological family when I knew that they were somewhere in the world but now I didn't even know if they were alive or if they'd been vanished, I felt a great wrench. They had put themselves in danger for my friend and I and hadn't really appreciated it. I had spent most of my time with them mired in doubt. I had questioned them constantly and I regretted it now. I was unsure if I would ever see either of them again. That made me feel strangely bereft. It had been a long time since my adoptive parents had died but with the disappearance of The Taxi Driver, it was like they'd died all over again. It was the feeling of loneliness being totally compounded.

I felt that I was on the outside of everything and looking down on it from a great height. I could see myself and Ellen and all of the other people involved in our lives and we were all like ants, scurrying around busying ourselves but then a great foot had appeared and was stamping on us all and grinding us into the dust until there was nothing left of anything. There was just a void. An empty space, just silence and darkness.

I looked at the garden with its garish colours and plasticity and thought what a dire contrast it was. It was hyper realistic. A glorious technicolour dreamscape where the flowers smelled of nothing and no wildlife called it their home. It was a lie. It was merely a flourescent deadscape. It was an approximation of a garden created by those who didn't love nature. It was only there to subdue and to subjugate. It could never provide any relief because those who created it didn't really care about it at all. They didn't care about soothing people with nature, it was just there as a means to an end. To gain an advantage of some kind. To get one over on those patients who were here to be controlled.

For a more naive person it was a means of trying to soften them up. A reward as opposed to the punishment of being drugged or subjected to the treatments that were being meted out in the secret control room. As I sat mulling over all of these things, I suddenly felt another low vibration alarm but this one was different. The light went off and I was in complete darkness. The vibration made me feel as though I'd been turned inside out and my bones had been shaken from their sockets. It was like being taken apart and being put back together again, backwards. Instead of the purple light that I'd seen before, this light glowed a pale orange. It felt more like an implosion than an explosion, as if everything had been reduced down into its core elements.

The trees seemed to shrink and reduce downwards.

I fell to the floor from the bench and laid flat, not daring to look up. The alarm created a tsunami of vibrations which seemed to swirl around and collapse everything down upon itself except for me. I tried to crawl forward but I was pinned to the ground. I wondered if it was some kind of nuclear explosion but there was no heat or fire and it seemed as if only the garden itself was being destroyed. None of it made any sense. I was scared for Ellen. Was something happening to her? I was sure that she would be absolutely terrified.

The orange light brightened suddenly and then dimmed. Everything went black and silent. I was conscious and found that I could move again. So, I stood up, trying to find my feet, tip toeing along, unsure whether the entire landscape had changed.

Then the lights came on. The garden had changed but not in the way that I had expected. There were no charred or collapsed benches or trees. Everything was as it was but had simply changed colour. I didn't know what had just happened but some enormous force had somehow moved in and changed everything.

****

CHAPTER 37

Once I'd moved from the garden, I walked into the corridor and at first didn't think that that much had changed. The wall, floor and ceiling were still a brilliant shade of white, as were the flourescent lights in the ceiling. And yet when I counted the doors, I noticed that there were six at each side instead of five. There were also two secret control rooms now instead of one, there were two, one at each side of the corridor.

"Why need another control room?" I thought. I didn't like the implication. If there were two control rooms it meant that were also two tables with restraints and two large screens made up of a puzzle of smaller screens, primed to broadcast orders regarding unknown treatments and modifications. It meant that two people could be treated simultaneously. Whether they intended now to treat me, I didn't know. I did know that I wouldn't go willingly and would do anything to avoid Stella and Nemo mucking around in my brain. I already knew what their intentions were.

But another thought did occur to me. Could it be that we had other patients arriving and so they needed to be made compliant so that they would fit in here. I didn't know which was actually worse, being at risk myself or thinking that there could be a production line of people being prepared for treatments that would convert them into automatons behind closed doors and that no one knew about it.

As yet, I hadn't seen any other patients arriving. I hadn't seen Ellen or any of the medical staff either. I resisted the urge to stick my head around Ellen's door to make sure that she was ok because I still didn't know where the cameras were or if the great realignment or whatever it was, had moved them into a different place altogether.

So, I continued on to my room to see if anything was any different there. There was nothing obvious immediately. The walls, floor and bed remained the same and yet when I looked up, the TV was a newer model and had been moved across to the other side of the room. I knew that there was likely to be some sort off broadcast imminently. As soon as I thought about it, it happened. Stella's face appeared once again.

"So, we have a few more patients. Many of you will be feeling confused as to what is happening and how you're to be here. You have been in suspended animation for a month. We had you removed because you were causing too much trouble and you wouldn't listen. I know that you likely don't believe a thing that I'm telling you. You probably don't believe that such technology exists, but really you should know better than that. You had access to many of our secrets and you've probably uncovered most of our plans already maybe even found ways to be able to disrupt them. So, we had to make sure that you couldn't do that. Our plans need to be carried out without any interference. You should take it as a compliment being here. You were a threat but that won't be the case while you're here."

I figured that this meant that the members of The Underground Resistance had been sent here. My heart leapt a bit. Maybe it meant that Nico and The Taxi Driver would be amongst them. At least I would know that they were alive if they were. But I was also saddened because I didn't want them to be subjected to the drugs and mental manipulation of the treatments. Nothing frightened me more than the fight going out of them all. They felt like some sort of last defence of decency, even if they weren't always so decent themselves. They stood against what was truly evil.

My mind drifted back to what Stella was saying.

"You will change while you are here. I will make sure of it. Whatever it takes. Whatever the consequences, you will be different when you leave here."

It was chilling. The true voice of the authoritarian. I hoped that any member of the resistance who was watching this would be as angry as I was. And yet I heard no noise or banging of hospital furniture in protest. There was just silence. I was sure that I could hear the voice of Stella echoing throughout the hospital. It reminded of those WW2 documentaries about Fascist dictators but instead of the roaring of the crowds, you could hear a pin drop.

A bit of me wondered if the resistance had even been sent here or if this was just another ruse to try and get inside my head. I hadn't seen anyone else or heard them. I'd only seen the change in the environment and now the usual spouted warning from Stella. Maybe it was all about me?

Then I had to stop it. I was getting ridiculously paranoid and off balance and that was giving Stella exactly what she wanted. Just another person unable to step up and go against her.

"Rounds will begin soon and then we'll begin our treatments. Most of you have tested positive for a virus so we'll need to give you medication to treat it. You'll need to stay in your isolation bubbles for a few weeks so that we can contain the outbreak." Stella said.

"You may feel a bit ill and drowsy to begin with. That's just the medication. It will pass. We'll put you to sleep if the infection becomes too bad or if you are unable to calm yourselves."

Stella finally stopped talking and the TV screen flashed off.

I was more determined than ever to sleep only at night. The rest of the time, I would record plan and investigate. I reached into my pocket and felt that the phone was still there. I turned the video camera on and made sure that my charger was close by.

I had no notepaper to make my records and my mind was too full to store anything else in, so I took the pillow case that I'd once stored my phone in and stuffed it into my pocket once more. I needed something to write but I could see no pens and didn't have any eyeliner pencils stashed anywhere either. I looked around to see if there were any medical notes with pens attached left anywhere but I couldn't see any. I then remembered that I could type in thoughts and prompts to my phone calendar but that I needed to come up with a number of code words so that even if my phone was intercepted, no one would know what they meant.

****

CHAPTER 38

Day?

I woke with a start. I was in the control room. I looked down and saw myself strapped to the table. I looked up and saw two masked medical staff leaning over me with some kind of device I didn't recognize. I looked at the end of the trolley and saw Stella.

"Why am I here? " I asked angrily " I've done everything you asked. I haven't gone against you and caused you problems." I said.

"But that's not true is it? You think that you can hide things from us, but we see everything." Said Stella.

"So just exactly what is it that I've done?" I asked

"Oh, you know. But I will list all of your transgressions if you like. You don't take your medications when we've expressly asked you too. We'll make sure that from now on all your drugs will be fed into your drip. You're trying to aggravate Ellen and encouraging her to rebel. She's already causing us problems but then you know that don't you?" Stella said.

"That's your problem isn't it? " I said " You can't accept that people have their own minds. Ellen has decided for herself that she doesn't like what's happening to her and won't accept what's going on here without a fight. I couldn't influence her if I wanted to. Yes, I haven't taken my medication because I didn't like what they were doing to me. I couldn't think."

"But I don't want you to think. I want you to obey. Remember you still work for me. I never did terminate your contract. You've just been on sick leave. "

Stella said.

I hadn't even thought about that. I'd been so caught up with recording what had been happening around the hospital and before that being in the bunker with the resistance, that it had totally slipped my mind. I was still an employee of Nemo and Co. I laughed and laughed, hysterically. The medical staff looked at one another slightly nervously unsure of what was going on. Stella remained impassive and simply waved her hand to signal that the treatment was to begin.

I heard a low hum as some kind of machinery that I couldn't see was switched on. The medical staff moved forwards and then rubbed something that I didn't recognize on my temples. The room began to glow purple. So, this is what the light is, I thought.

The nurse moved forwards with two cylindrical devices and placed them on either side of my head. The last thing I remembered thinking was, I hope I'm still the same person after all of this.

****

CHAPTER 39

Day?

The light was a blur when I came round and the only way, I could describe my mind was that it was rather like a jigsaw puzzle that had a couple of pieces missing. Everything seemed upside down and back to front. A nurse was stood at the end of my bed and looked at me quizzically.

"How are you feeling now? "She asked.

"I'm not sure" I said. "A bit confused really."

"Well, that's understandable. You've only just had some treatment." She said.

I noticed that there was another figure sat in the chair next to my bedside. They seemed vaguely familiar but I couldn't get my brain together enough to actually recognize who it was. They studied me closely to see if there was any recognition.

"You don't remember me at all do you? " She said.

I looked more carefully. She was a dark-haired woman, around my age, maybe slightly younger than me. I could see an image of her in my mind's eye speaking on a screen or maybe performing on a stage in front of lots of people. But further than that, I didn't know. All I could see was a few unrelated images that didn't seem to fit together. I didn't remember how they did.

"Don't worry." The woman said." You're tired. I'll come back when you've recovered from the treatment a bit more."

She nodded to the nurse and then walked out of the room. I felt sad as I watched her leave. She must have been important in my life but I didn't know why. I wondered how long the amnesia would last. I couldn't remember much just a purple light and then waking up later.

"I'll leave you alone for a little bit to recuperate." The nurse said.

"Then I'll come back later to ask you some questions. Do you want the TV leaving on?"

"Ok." I said.

I looked at the screen but was having trouble taking anything in. It was as if the images made it as far as my eyes but then became absent of any sense once it crossed over to my brain. I could see the pictures but they had no meaning at all. I knew what they were but couldn't give them any context. A red route master bus with the roof coming apart from it. An ambulance then an insert with photographs of two men, one wearing a security guard's uniform. The other had a craggy face. He seemed to be in late middle age. I recognized both of them but it was the older man who I felt a feeling of fondness for, though I didn't know why.

Adverts kept popping up for various things. Lots of financial stuff, many featuring a man, a balding, sneering, curmudgeon, who patently looked down on everyone. I just kept hearing the same voice going round and round in my head. Stella, Stella, Stella.

I couldn't put a face to the name, but I knew that it was important. Maybe Stella was the woman who had been sat at the side of my bed. Whoever she was, I wasn't sure but my brain kept repeating the name over and over and all I knew was that I didn't have a good feeling about it. Not at all.

****

The confusion in my brain rolled away like clouds parting. When I looked up, I looked into the eyes in the centre of a metal face. I recognized at once who Stella was. She just looked at me with no expression.

"Why are you stood there?" I yelled climbing out of bed and

rushing towards her. "Why are you trying to erase me? Why are you trying to change me and tell lies about me?"

I don't know what I was trying to achieve. Pretty difficult to win against a seven-foot-tall chrome robot. I couldn't rush her of course. I didn't have the strength. She stuck her hand out and picked me up by the throat and I felt like a child in a cartoon kicking out at the villain as my legs ran through the air. Unfortunately, though I was kicking at nothing and as Stella pulled me level with her eye line, my vulnerability was compounded.

"You have got to learn." Stella said. "It's just not possible for you to go against us. You're just not thinking straight if you think that you can. I only have to send you off for a treatment and any ideas that you get into your head about not behaving properly while you're in here will vanish."

I knew it was fruitless but I just kept kicking at the air. I was so angry that it fused into my bones. Stella just dropped me to the floor and laughed. I crumpled slightly as I was winded through being dropped so suddenly from a great height. Stella walked off towards the door slowly and then turned around to face me.

"Keep trying." She mocked. "It gives me something to do."

After she'd gone, I sat on the floor and cried. I looked at the bed and then at the chair and finally at the floor. How did I keep going? At that moment I felt broken. I no longer knew what was real and what was a dream. Everything seemed to meld together. It was just one big mess. How had I ever got into this situation and how would I get out of it? It seemed that wherever I looked, all of the exits were closed. And yet, I couldn't give up. Not yet. I couldn't just give in to Stella's demands. I couldn't let myself be ground down into despair. I had to keep going, whatever it took.

****

CHAPTER 40

Day?

When people are imprisoned, in order to survive they need a purpose and a routine. I had deduced that I may be in a hospital but to all intents and purposes, I was in a prison. To an extent, I was already institutionalised. I suppose I had got used to the comings and goings of the medical staff, the supervised exercise and now, the brain scrambling sessions. I was relieved to note that after the initial forgetfulness and confusion, everything came back fairly rapidly and sometimes more strongly than before. It was as if my brain was getting used to it, even maybe becoming immune. Knowing that in spite of her best efforts, that Stella was failing in her mission to try to erase me gave me a great deal of satisfaction.

****

I began to feel like two different people. The one who performed like a seal to keep the all-seeing eyes happy and Stella off my back, then the second inner person who was the real, authentic me. In order to start my new routine, I knew that I needed to be as mentally and physically fit as possible. So, every morning I walked. I walked from my bed to the garden and then once in the garden, I did circuits in order to walk 5,000 steps. I counted each and every step in my head. I noticed that the medical staff were curious. But I think they were happy to encourage me in what seemed a genuine interest in my physical health.

I also decided to ask for a number of puzzle books. This was to serve a dual purpose. To sharpen my mind firstly, but also to help me consider code names for my record keeping. I could use the books themselves as ways of recording what was currently happening and what I intended to do I the future and no one would be any the wiser. I would be the only one who knew what each code word meant. So, the records would be hidden in plain sight. I was also fairly sure that no one would be overly suspicious if I just spent a bit of time everyday filling in puzzle books. It was just wily enough for me to feel rather pleased with myself.

Sure enough, the day after I asked for them, the puzzle books arrived with a pencil. They obviously thought that the pencil was less capable of causing damage than a pen. I'm also sure that they thought that it would be harder for me to write on other things, if I only had a pencil to play with. That was fine, it was good enough.

So, every day, I engaged with my new routine. Walking 5,000 steps in the morning and completing the puzzle books in the afternoon. I found that my vocabulary was broadening quickly and the medical staff seemed more than happy that I was seemingly engaging with hospital life more constructively. My outer self was so reassuring well behaved, the ultimate good patient, while my inner self was rebelling away nicely.

I'd noticed that I hadn't had another visit from the dark-haired woman. I wondered if she'd come back but I still couldn't remember who she was. I also noticed that there were no other patients in the hospital. I was sure that I'd had a vague memory of others but I just couldn't remember who they were. It just seemed very strange being in an entirely empty hospital. I wondered how long it would stay that way. Maybe I was the only one that they had failed to reeducate? I very much hoped not.

****

4 down-A bad tempered person, often but not always an older one,10 letters, beginning with c and ending with n. Curmudgeon, I thought. That'll suit Mr. Nemo nicely.

6 across and 10 down-title of a song by Radiohead, first word, beginning with a p,8 letters second word letter a,7 letters. I

smiled. Paranoid Android, well that's Stella alright. It was quite fun thinking up all of the code words. 12 down-7 letters a domestic or industrial worker who cleans houses or commercial premises. Second meaning, fixers who specialize in getting rid of evidence e.g., Bodies. Beginning with cleaner, that's me I thought and then considered how both meanings were quite appropriate. Though even though I may have aided with the getting rid of evidence, I hadn't as yet got rid of any bodies and I hoped I never would.

Finally, an apocalyptic event, the end times. Beginning with an a. 10 letters. I scratched my head for a moment and then thought how truly right the word was for my plan, the code for bringing down Nemo and decommissioning Stella. "Armageddon."

****

It's amazing how quickly you can become fit, if you really put your mind to it.

My walking regime was working and I found that I was becoming stronger and stronger both physically and mentally. Focusing was becoming easier and I was even wondering whether the drugs that the medical staff had been giving me had been discontinued. After the first few, I hadn't had any more treatments in the medical room either that I could remember but I wasn't a hundred per cent sure. I still had a drip but maybe that was only a saline drip to stop me from becoming dehydrated.

I realized that aside from my florid dreams, I hadn't seen any sign of Stella either in person or on the TV screen for a few days. The strange programmes that had been made by Nemo and Stella seemed to have been replaced by more conventional fare. Programmes about renovating houses or gritty soaps with dramatic storylines. It was all becoming rather mundane and boring but it made a nice change. It seemed as though my life has been a constant roller coaster as long as I could remember and it was only now that I had actually stopped for a short time that I was really beginning to recognize it.

Still, beneath the surface, I knew that all was not as it seemed. I watched the soaps for fun. I didn't really like them much but I noticed that there were actors who looked like Nemo and even Stella, without the chrome. They seemed to pop up again and again in various guises in the renovation programmes, on a shopping channel even in a cookery programme.

I wondered at first if I'd imagined it or if it was yet another way of trying to psyche me out. Maybe it was just a coincidence or maybe it was an incidence of when you see a likeness, you just can't let go of it. And so, it went through every advert and programme for the next few days. I saw facsimiles of Nemo and Stella everywhere. Buy a new car and Nemo is selling it. The weather report and Stella is the presenter. I wondered if I was going mad and seeing things. I didn't think it was wise to mention it to the medical staff. So, I decided to keep it to myself. I made sure to make a note of it using my code words in the puzzle books. The books at least never seemed to be looked at or investigated so I could write pretty much whatever I wanted in there. They were in code and so to anyone else they would've just seemed incoherent and so they wouldn't have bothered.

****

Day?

It must've been a few days later when I was filling in my puzzle book, looking for new code words, when one of the medical staff popped their head around the door.

"You have a visitor." They said.

I looked up and noticed that the dark-haired woman was walking in to the room.

"Do you remember who I am yet?" She asked.

When I looked at her, I saw an image of a man on a bus. He'd tried to give me something and something bad had happened to him but I couldn't remember what. She was something to do with him. I thought.

"I remember your face," I said "But I don't remember you. I'm sorry."

"Don't worry." She replied. "You've been through a lot."

"I do remember something else though." I said " I remember a man's face and he had something to do with you?"

She smiled slightly and sat down on one of the chairs next to the bed.

"Well, that's good that you've started to remember us a bit. I've brought another visitor with me too" She said and motioned to another figure who was hovering in the doorway.

It was an older man. He looked familiar too, but he wasn't the man who I associated with the woman.

"Hello babe, remember me?" He asked in a broad cockney accent.

"Sort of." I said "I know your face, like hers but I don't know how I know you. I'm sorry."

He looked a bit disappointed but gave a slight smile anyway. The nurse who had been hovering slightly in the background spoke up.

"Amnesia's fairly common after what she's been through. Just take it slowly and don't be too disappointed that she doesn't know who you are just yet."

The older man and dark-haired woman just nodded and sat either side of the bed. The man looked at me quizzically.

"You really don't remember me at all babe?" He asked.

I looked at him very carefully. I saw a few things when I looked at him. I saw an ambulance and also a taxi. We were driving together through the city in both vehicles.

"You drive a taxi and I've been in it a few times." I said.

"Yes, babe that is true." He said." Do you remember anything else?"

"We've been in an ambulance and there was a security guard. Something happened to him, I think." I said.

The man looked at the woman. I found their expressions difficult to read. Simultaneously, they grabbed a hand each.

"Listen" the woman said. "It's the first time you've seen each other in quite a while so try not to worry. Things can get quite jumbled up in your brain with what you've been through. Not to mention the treatment here. So, try not to upset yourself. It'll all come back to you when you're ready and we can keep coming to visit you, to try to help you remember."

"Ok." I said "But can I ask you a question?"

"Yes, whatever you want." She said.

"I just keep noticing that I'm the only patient here. My friend Ellen was here, then she went for a treatment one day and disappeared. Apart from both of you and the medical staff, I haven't seen anyone else since." I said.

The woman looked at me carefully and didn't say anything to begin with. She didn't seem to really know what to say.

"We can come again to see you tomorrow." She said.

"But you didn't answer the question." I said . "Are there any other patients here and what happened to Ellen? Why won't you tell me?" I said.

"Don't upset yourself." She said "We'll come back tomorrow and then we'll talk about it it, I promise." The woman then patted my hand and left the room. The man smiled at me and squeezed my other hand.

"See you tomorrow, babe." He said "You're doing really well."

He then took a long hard look at me then followed the dark-haired woman out of the door. They were keeping things from me. It was obvious but I didn't know why and I couldn't see any reason for them not answering my questions.

I felt that I needed to look through my puzzle book to find some appropriate code words for them to add to my records. I flicked through the pages quickly, hoping to find the correct words. I kept looking and looking but most of the clues didn't seem to fit. Then on the last page of the last book I found them. 8 down - slang name for a city taxi driver beginning with c. 6 letters.

"Cabbie." I said out loud and then looked around to see that no one was listening.

Yes, that was right, I thought. I just needed another word or phrase to describe the woman. 6 across, female sibling,6 letters beginning with s.

"Oh my God." I said "She's my sister."

****

CHAPTER 41

Day?

So, I'd remembered that the dark-haired woman was my sister and the man was a cabbie but I knew that there were lots of other things that I couldn't remember properly. Images rose and fell in my head like balloons. I still remembered the other man and wanted to ask about him. I hadn't seen Stella and Nemo again. I'd only seen their look alike on the various tv shows and adverts.

When I went for my usual morning walk, I decided to explore a little bit to see what I could find out. I wanted to see if there actually were any other patients and also what had happened to Ellen seeing as no one wanted to tell me anything. I got out of bed and wandered down the corridor towards the garden. As I walked down the corridor, I noticed that there were no longer six doors on either side and it seemed to go on for longer. I also noticed that there were no longer two control rooms. Now there was only one. I looked around to see if there was anyone watching then I tried the door. It was locked. I continued on walking until I reached the double doors. The garden was no longer there, just another corridor.

I noticed a porter, someone I hadn't seen before, pushing an empty wheelchair towards a lift that I also hadn't seen before.

"Could you tell me where the garden is please?" I asked.

"Yes certainly." He said " It's just at the end of this corridor and through the double doors."

"Thanks." I said and then paused for a moment.

"Have you worked here for long? I've never seen you before." I asked.

"Oh yes." He said " I've been here for ten years now. Maybe you just haven't seen me because I don't work on your ward. Which ward are you on?"

I pointed to the double doors behind me. He pulled a strange face but then very quickly smiled and spoke to me very kindly as someone would to a small child.

"That explains it then." He said. "I don't work on there. You go and have a nice walk in the garden. The fresh air will do you good." He then disappeared into the lift pushing the empty wheelchair.

I pushed through the double doors and found myself outside in an actual garden. I was completely taken aback and it felt as though the floor was moving around under my feet. I found a bench to sit down on and steadied myself. I could smell the heady scent of roses in the air and birdsong filled my ears in God only knows how long. I closed my eyes and took it all in. It was a welcome bit of peace and normality amid the recent chaos that my life had become.

When I opened my eyes again, I felt like I was being looked at. I looked around and noticed that there were indeed other patients in the garden but I didn't recognize any of them. They were smoking, reading or even chatting with other visitors. A few of them stared at me in a rather hostile manner and spoke behind their hands so that I couldn't work out what they were saying. That had answered one of my questions but not the other one about Ellen and where she was.

I got up and walked over to one of the patients who was reading and asked them if they knew an Ellen. They simply shook their head, didn't look up and carried on reading. I approached someone else and the response was the same. I carried on until I'd asked each and every person in the garden. Not one of them knew anything.

Frustrated, I went back inside and dashed up through the first set of double doors and noticed that the control room door was open. I moved my way quickly towards it and looked inside. It was some kind of cleaning supplies room and in the corner was a man filling up his cleaning trolley.

"Oi, what're you doing in here?" He said and started to come towards me. There were no TV screens or gurneys with hand and ankle ties. There were only mops and industrial sized bottles of bleach. Nothing else.

"What's going on?" I yelled." Where are the screens and the machines?"

The man looked puzzled and a little bit afraid. He just stayed where he was and put his hands out in front of him in a pacifying gesture.

"It's ok. It's ok." He said gently." You're just not supposed to be in here."

"Where's it all gone?" I screamed " I know you've hidden it all. And where's Ellen, what have you done with her?"

The man-made quiet shushing sounds and then looked behind me slightly. Before I could turn around, I felt a sharp pain in my neck and then all too soon, I blacked out.

****

CHAPTER 42

Day?

When I came round, I was in the ward again propped up in bed with both The Taxi Driver and my sister sitting either side of the bed.

"I remember who you are." I said. "You're my sister and you're The Taxi Driver." I pointed at each of them. They both looked quite pleased that I now seemed to know at least a little bit about who they were.

"I am a Taxi Driver." The man said. "But not only that, I'm your Dad too."

I looked at him and then had a vague recollection of having had this chat before.

"Yes, I remember that now. We were talking in the bunker before you all disappeared. I'd only just got to know you all and then you all vanished into thin air and I ended up here. So did Ellen. Where is Ellen? I keep asking about her and nobody will tell me anything. The patients, Doctors, even you. Nothing." Dad and my sister both held my hand and Dad said.

"We thought that you were getting so much better. Ok let's talk about Ellen."

****

I sat up in bed and screwed a tissue up under my eyes to catch the tears that were constantly falling.

"What do you remember?" Dad said.

"Not much. Ellen had been pushed in front of a car just outside the flat. She told me that when she was here. She also told me that she couldn't remember anything between being hit by the car and us moving her in the ambulance."

Dad looked at my sister and didn't say anything.

"Don't you remember Netty pushed Lawson out of the window because he was trying to attack Ellen to get to me. We came to pick her up out of intensive care and drove her in an ambulance to a private hospital run by The Underground Resistance. You accidentally hit a security guard who tried to shoot at us when we were driving away."

Dad looked ashen faced and held my hand.

"Oh love." He said. " I don't know how to tell you this. It's really difficult."

"What is it? " I said, looking at the pained expression on his face. " Did something happen to her? Did she die?" I gulped and gasped as I couldn't stop myself from crying hysterically.

"She didn't die here. "He said. "Can I go and see her, wherever she is?" I asked

"No, you can't go to see her." He said gently.

"Why not? Is it because I've got to stay here."? I said becoming agitated again.

"No babe, it isn't that at all. Ellen doesn't exist. Not anymore anyway. She was your best friend when you were a child but she was hit by a car on her way walking home from your birthday party when you were eight. She was your imaginary friend for a few years after and then you didn't see her for years and years. Then your partner was killed in a bus bombing when he was working for Nemo and Co abroad. After that happened, you started hallucinating because you were so grief stricken. You kept seeing Ellen and other things. " Dad said.

"What are you talking about?" I shouted.

"Ellen is real. I spoke to her while I was in that weird plastic garden that used to exist where those double doors are now."

Dad just shook his head.

"That was a hallucination too as was the garden." He said.

"I don't believe you. Why would you say shit like that to me? What about my partner? I haven't had one for years. What did he look like?" I said.

My sister rummaged around in her bag and got out a crumpled photograph and then lay it on the bed for me to have a look at.

"That's him, David." She said. " I'm really sorry this must be very upsetting for you."

I looked closely at the photo. It was the pallid man who had been killed on the bus. He was the one who'd passed the note to me asking for help. I knew that he wasn't my partner because I had felt absolutely nothing at all for him. I could remember that much. Also, I was fairly certain that if you loved a person so deeply that you hallucinated when they were killed, you would at least feel something when you saw their photo.

"But he wasn't my husband, Nico." I said. " He was yours."

My sister looked at me with an expression of disbelief.

"My name isn't Nico. It's Nicky and he wasn't my husband, he was yours." She started to get angry and gripped my hand slightly tighter. My Dad shook his head at her and she loosened her grip slightly.

"He wasn't called David. He was called Cale Reed. He was killed in a bus bombing but not anywhere abroad, it was right here in the city. He was trying

to expose experiments and he needed my help. Why are you pretending that none of this ever happened?" I said.

My sister pushed her chair right back until it screeched along the floor and banged against the wall.

"Dad I can't do this anymore. I don't think she's getting any better. In fact, I think she's getting worse." She said then got up and walked out slamming the ward door behind her. My dad just sat there and shook his head sadly.

"Don't worry love." He said " Just you take your time to get better. There's no rush. Don't mind your sister. She just gets frustrated because she's worried about you. She don't mean anything by it."

He ruffled my hair slightly and then got up.

"I got you some chocolate peanuts love. I know they're your favourite. " He said and then dropped a bag full on the bed side table.

"Thanks Dad." I said and put them in the locker. I waved at him as he made his way through the door. Once he'd gone, I threw the peanuts straight in the bin. I knew for certain then that they had been lying to me. I was allergic to peanuts and anyone who knew me well enough would know that.

My gut instinct told me to get out of bed and look out of the window. I peeked carefully out from behind the curtains and I saw my Dad and sister talking to what appeared to be a 7ft tall chrome figure. Now I knew that they were all in it together, but for the life of me, I didn't know why.

****

I sat in bed and had so many questions. They went over and over in my mind. The man who said that he was my Dad obviously wasn't. Neither was the person who said she was my sister a relative either. Somehow, they had managed to encourage me to trust them and then encouraged me to try to believe that I was actually going mad. It seemed that both Nemo and Co. and The Underground Resistance were all part and parcel of the same plot.

I felt sure now that Ellen was around here somewhere and she was being kept away from me deliberately. But why? It seemed that there was no one here that I could trust. If only I could find Ellen and talk to her again. I felt that yet again, I was going to have to play another character to try to find out what was really happening and yet at the same time hide the fact that I knew that Nico and The Taxi Driver were in cahoots with Nemo and Co.

At that moment, a note was posted underneath the door. I tip-toed over to it and picked it up. I got back into bed and opened it up under the covers, in case either the medical staff or anyone else came in.

It read;

"You're right to be suspicious. Very little here is as it seems. If you think you're being used as part of an experiment, you're on the right track. The USB you smuggled out from Nemo and Co is genuine. Believe it. There are many people who are conspiring against you, but don't despair. You have friends. I'm not dead. I'm here to help."

It was signed Cale Reed.

****

CHAPTER 43

So, Cale Reed was neither dead nor my husband. It seemed he was either working here somewhere in the bowels of this hospital or had slipped in, masquerading as a visitor somehow. He'd obviously managed to fly under the radar and managed not to be rumbled either by the staff or Stella.

It meant that he'd been alive the whole time he'd been reported as dead. It was shocking and strange to report him as dead especially in the way he had supposedly died but it fit in entirely with Nemo and Co's changing of the facts on an industrial scale. I just didn't understand why? I was now looking forward to actually meeting him properly.

And yet there was a part of me that wondered if this was yet another strategy or scheme to unbalance me. Have someone write a letter posing as Cale Reed to draw me out and see what I would do. I hid the letter away between the pages of my puzzle book. I knew that I must find a code word for Cale now to add him to the record.

I beavered through my books looking for the most appropriate words. It was strange. I'd only met him once for the briefest of moments on the bus but he was a significant part of what had happened to me in these last few weeks. There was something about him that meant he was the key to everything that was happening and it was obviously essential to find out what it was.

As I looked through my books, I ticked and rejected a number of code words. None of them seemed quite right. Then as I turned over the page it suddenly leaped out at me.

9 down,8 letters beginning with L and ending with n. The central idea or cornerstone. Linchpin, for whatever reason, Cale Reed was the linchpin and I had to find out the reason why.

****

In the middle of the night, I woke up with a start, there was a figure I didn't recognize at the end of my bed. They were almost completely covered in shadow. Only the pale light from the street light outside leaked through the window. It gave the figure a sort of glimmering halo. I didn't know if it was a good idea to pretend that I was still asleep or to acknowledge their presence. I realized that it couldn't be Stella. They weren't tall enough. If it were one of the medical staff there to wheel me off for treatment, undoubtedly, they would've just taken me away without any fanfare at all. They certainly wouldn't have just lurked there in the darkness at the end of my bed.

"Are you awake? " A man's voice whispered. " Did you get my note?"

So, it was Cale Reed. How had he got in? The ward was usually closed after ten o' clock to prevent any midnight wandering and yet here he was.

"Yes, and yes." I said. " I'm very confused. How did you get in? Do you work here now?"

"Yes" he said. " We have a lot to discuss. I still need your help, if you'll help me."

"Yes, I will help you." I said " But there's an awful lot of things I want to know from you first."

****

It is a peculiar thing sitting and talking to a man in the middle of the night that you thought was dead. He came and sat down on the end of my bed and I looked at him trying to remember if he looked like the actual Cale Reed that I'd met before. The light was fairly dim but I did recognize the contours of his face. It's hard to forget the face of a person that you believe had been killed in such a brutal way. They become indelibly imprinted on your brain.

"I don't really know you at all," I said " but I'm glad that you're ok. What actually happened?"

I looked at him carefully and the only things that were different were that his hair was slightly longer and he had the beginnings of a beard. His pallid face shone slightly in the dim light.

"I don't have long. They start doing rounds again at 6 am so we've only got a couple of hours. Firstly, before I tell you what you want to know, I've swapped your pills for sugar tablets and your drip is only a saline drip now. If you hadn't guessed already, they've been trying to fill you full of Finax. One of Nemo's drugs. The idea being to keep your brain cloudy and make money off you." He said.

"Well, what a surprise." I said and raised my eyebrows." Thanks."

"So, the last time we met on the bus, I gave you a note, which you obviously found." He said.

I just nodded.

"After I got off the bus, I stopped for a coffee and then walked home. By the time I got in, I saw on the news that I was already dead, killed in the bus bombing. Once I saw this, I knew that I'd have to go to ground because Stella would be sending Lawson and his cleaning team with a syringe full of Finax or some other narcotic to finish me off within a matter of minutes. So, I took an emergency rucksack full of only the bare essentials. Whatever I could carry. I had known that this would happen sooner or later, so I already had an escape plan prepared just in case. I needed to disappear quickly and as far as possible without a trace. So, I had my burner phone, a wedge of cash and a flask. The rest I could work out en route." He said.

"The hardest bit was being able to avoid the cctv cameras because they're everywhere now. Thankfully one of the perks of working for Mr. Nemo is that it's possible to map at least most of the official ones. There are of course loads of cars with dash cams and private properties with their own cameras. But still they're often of a lower quality and so even if I showed up on one of those, they couldn't necessarily identify me.

So, I'd worked out a route ahead of time, on foot, to go and see one of two hackers I knew. Both lived off grid. I knew it would only be a matter of time before one of them would be tracked down, once they'd realized that I'd disappeared. I got to the first. He lived closest, still in the city. I looked through his window and saw him hanging from his ceiling light. His place was turned completely upside down. It was obviously Stella's work. I was completely unsurprised. But what did surprise me was that there was no one still hanging around. I assumed that there was some sort of surveillance set up there to try to catch me out. I didn't go in and to my shame, I didn't call 999 straightaways either.

I did call his mother though and told her I was a friend who was worried about him and to maybe give him a call. I hope she called the police. I hope that she didn't go round and I find him herself. It's a sight no mother should have to see."

He stopped for a moment and took a deep breath. I looked at him and thought that he'd aged a lot since I'd seen him last. Just like he had the weight of the world on his shoulders. He began talking again.

"I walked out of the city overnight, keeping to the side roads and then managed to get to the squat where my second hacker friend was living. If you didn't know that anyone is living there you would miss it as it just seems to be a condemned property in the middle of nowhere. I was glad to find that he was ok and hadn't been discovered yet. He had a lead lined underground basement, a relic from the 1918 pandemic. Apparently, it had been some sort of spare mortuary in the peak of the pandemic. It seemed that we couldn't stay in there long because of the lead, so we set up new identities as quickly as we could. I got a buzz cut and a fake beard just until I had enough time to grow a new one and we both took off.

I flew way under the radar staying in derelict beach huts or in homemade shelters deep in the woods. I foraged for food and sometimes rifled through the bins of supermarkets late at night. By the second week I was quite amazed that they hadn't found me. But I decided that I needed to see what they had done regarding my supposed death in the bus bombing. So, on one of my bin raiding missions, I pinched a newspaper from a stack that had been left on the doorstep of a village shop. No one noticed and I sat down behind the beach hut trying to figure out what had been going on in my absence. Even I was surprised by the audacity of it.

They had decided to get rid of me officially but more than that they decided to make me a terrorist too. Kill me off and then smear me too while they were at it. They even went as far as to invent me a wife and put on a press conference with her."

I looked puzzled. It hadn't occurred to me that Nico and him weren't actually married at all.

"So, you're not married to Nico. Do you even know her?" I asked.

" Oh yes, I know her." He said.

"We worked together in the intelligence department of Nemo and Co. She was a specialist in advanced robotics and I was involved in the finance department."

"So that bit was true at least." I said. " I know Nico and The Taxi Driver quite well. They recruited me to The Underground Resistance after you died, sorry, were supposed to have died."

"Yes, I know. Nico was always loyal to the company first and foremost because she believed in what they were trying to do. In some warped way, she believed that she was doing the right thing for human kind. She thought that the creation of Stella and the other elements of experimenting on the population meant that weaker elements were being weeded out and that humanity would be strengthened."

I let out a long sigh.

"That sounds an awful lot like eugenics, the exact opposite of what she told me. I never did 100 per cent trust her though." I said.

"You're a wise woman." Cale said."

"She told me that she'd invented Stella and that she had decided to create the underground resistance because she didn't agree with the way that her utopian ideas had been stolen and misrepresented by Nemo and co. So obviously that wasn't true either." I said.

"Ha! Oh, where to start." Cale said and laughed bitterly. " I told you that I knew her from working together. I was always quite wary of her as she had quite strange ideas. She was a bit of an ideologue. She wanted to invent an android enforcer to enable the experiments that had been directed by governments and heads of states to occur. She believed that at the point of enforcement, basically the suppression and murder of any one resistant to the plan, the great majority of human kind will be repulsed and find reasons not to do it. There exceptions but she believed that people are to capricious and emotional to do what she felt needed to be done. The whole point of Stella, regardless of her trying to tell you otherwise, was to eliminate any opposition. That was the pinnacle of her scientific work. She was the most dangerous kind of ideologue because she believed so strongly that what she was doing was morally superior, that she would do anything to ensure that it would happen. "

"So, the ends justify the means. She did say that to me once." I said.

" Yes, I bet she did." said Cale.

I sat there thinking quietly for a moment. A part of me felt vindicated for being skeptical of Nico all along. My judgement of character remained largely intact but at the same time it was a chilling realization that ultimately my gut feelings were correct. This person had posed as my sister merely to attempt to use me as a patsy and smear me.

"Carry on." I said " I want to know how you managed to get here."

"Well, once they had told the media that I was the one responsible for the bus bombing and that I was dead, I knew that I had to lay low for a while. It's harder than it looks but I did have support. It was just tricky being able to access it. After I nicked the newspaper and knew the score, I knew that I had to keep moving and contact some of the other ex-Nemo and Co. workers who had been through similar and had to go to ground before me." He said.

"There's others?" I asked.

"Oh yes. Most of them have been smeared as terrorists or addicts and then reported as dead. Any stories that you may have read or seen on the evening news about the underground resistance and its associates who have committed any murders or robberies in their name you can safely conclude that they were working against Nemo from within the company and that they've either been killed or had to go on the run.

There was a woman ,it was quite a high-profile story, she'd been supposedly found dead in her flat of an overdose. Then much was made of how she was in fact a drug runner for the resistance." Cale said.

"Was that Jane? The Taxi Driver's daughter?" I interrupted.

"Indeed." said Cale "but she was neither dead or The Taxi Driver's daughter. She'd had a similar experience to me. She'd been a personal assistant for Nemo and even featured in some of his promotional material. He assumed that she was a total supporter of his and so he gave her intimate access to a lot of the robotics information. I think he also likely thought that she wasn't intelligent enough to understand what she was reading. He was mistaken of course because Jane has a degree in Maths and originally went to work for Nemo because she, like me had been taken in by the advertising but also sadly like me, was dazzled by the prestige and money bestowed upon us by working for a large corporation. Once she had seen what was happening there, she knew she couldn't live with being a part of it. She was the first out of all of us to try to get the message out. She tried to smuggle out some documents related to the potential experiments and Stella's role. But before she could leak them to the press, Nemo pulled his usual trick and published the news that she was not only dead but also a drug runner. With the aid of a few disguises, she managed to disappear and found herself in an isolated cottage up in the highlands. It was where I was headed after Nemo killed me off. She'd been following the news and so been expecting me since she'd seen the reports of the bus bombing. When it's happened to you, you know what to look for. She'd managed to keep hold of some of the documents that she'd smuggled out and one of them featured a secret hospital established by Nemo. Outwardly it purported to be a rehabilitation and mental health clinic but that was merely a front enabling the company to carry out its population experiments using Finax. She was fairly sure that she'd be able to infiltrate the hospital and be hired as a nurse."

"That was a pretty risky idea." I said " Because surely she could be recognized?"

"Yes, but remember apart from people in the know, most people would think she was dead. Most of the medical staff wouldn't have had a clue because they wouldn't have met her when she worked in Nemo's office. However, that said, as it turned out, there was one nurse who did recognize her. She was also filmed in some of the promotional material but she was very amenable to helping both Jane and I to infiltrate the building. Nemo had been holding her children and her husband hostage, she absolutely loathes him." Cale said.

"Yes, I overheard that. I managed to sneak into the control room once and heard him say that." I said.

"Well then so you've heard with your own ears what a bully and manipulator he is. He uses people's weaknesses against them. But there's also a risk in doing that to people. Eventually they get sick of it and start to rebel in different ways, either overtly or covertly." Cale said.

"So, are you telling me that there are three of you here who are now actively working against Nemo?" I said.

"Yes." Cale said. " You may have found that slowly but surely your mind is becoming less foggy. If any of the three of us are on shift we've been swapping the Finax and changing your drip. So, there are three of us looking after you but we're in the minority. The majority of staff still have complete loyalty to Nemo. You need to be really careful."

I sat there thinking for a moment.

"Do you know anything about my friend, Ellen?" I asked.

"Yes." Cale said.

"Is she still here and is she safe?" I asked.

"She is still here." He said " But she's not really safe. Nemo knows that she's your Achilles heel. So just like the others, he's trying to harm her to get to you. She's in the isolation unit at the moment. During the day he's brainwashing her and he's going to use it as a means to get to you. She's in quite a bad way. She's not coping very well, and he knows that that will really hurt you. We've been trying to get into the unit when we can to try to mitigate what he's doing to her but it's quite tough. The security is stricter around there."

I shook my head. I was appalled at the utter cruelty of it. There seemed to be a complete lack of humanity at the heart of Nemo.

"What is it that they are wanting me to do?" I asked " Do you have any idea?"

"Yes, they've already set the ground work for it by painting you as a terrorist and murderer. Hence the news stories. They are going to try to do to you what they've done to me but even worse. They are going to try to force you to go into a public place and blow yourself up." He said.

"You're to act as a cover. They are going to perform one of their experiments by using a pathogen on a designated area. All significant figures will be evacuated ahead of time or inoculated. By using you to do it, you will be both the means of delivery and the dead cat who distracts the public from the reality of what's actually happening."

I drew a sharp intake of breath.

"Bloody hell." I said. " So, they're basically going to use Ellen as blackmail to try to force me into doing it. Shit, this is so evil on so many levels. I can't get my head around it all."

Cale nodded quietly.

"It's understandable considering it's like something that you'd read in a book. But I assure you that it's very real. But this is why I wanted to speak to you to reassure you that you have us to back you up, but also to give you a heads up to prepare yourself."

"Do you know when they're going to try and approach me?" I asked.

"Likely tomorrow. There's likely to be something contained within one of those programmes or adverts that Stella so enjoys torturing us all with. Keep your eyes open for those. It's likely that they may try to insert some footage of Ellen or use some other way to get to you. I'm sorry this is really distressing but hold fast because we're trying to find ways to disrupt what's happening. We're going to try our best to get Ellen out." Cale said.

"But will she be safe? " I asked. " I don't want her to be in any danger."

"We won't put her in any danger and once she's away from the treatments and the Finax , she'll be fine." Cale said "She may need weaning off and that won't be easy. She may have withdrawals but we'll look after her."

"Your letter said that you needed my help but so far you haven't said how I can help." I said.

Cale took a deep breath.

" Basically, I need you to play along. To begin we need Nemo to think that you'll do what he asks without too much resistance and then once you're sure that he believes you, you need to record everything so we can use it to present to the media. Then we'll be able to stop them from carrying out these experiments once and for all." Cale said.

I sat there trying to take everything in. I couldn't believe what I was hearing. In the space of a month, I had gone from being a cleaner to a potential suicide bombers and biological weapon under duress.

"Can I ask something else?" I said.

"Yes. Anything." Cale said.

" We never got to the bottom of how Nico, The Taxi Driver and the underground resistance fit into all of this." I said.

"Ah yes," Cale said. "That is the clever or truly villainous bit, depending on your point of view. Nemo and Stella wanted to create an outfit that could serve as fall guys when the bombing took place in order to allow them to keep their noses clean. There may be may be many powerful individuals caught up in all of this but if it's public knowledge that they're responsible for carrying out experiments on their own people, they wouldn't last very long. So, they needed to create a shadow organization to take the blame. They needed to do this gradually in order to make it seem legitimate but it also served as a useful way to get rid of any individual who either found out about their plans or tried to frustrate them. See yours truly."

I nodded.

"They've created this shadow organization especially to be responsible?" I asked " They're playing both sides, like Finax and the rehab centres."

"Exactly." Cale said." They also went further than that. They recruited you with the sole purpose of making you the fall guy. They were fishing around for people on online recruitment websites. Looking for people with vulnerabilities. Specific behaviour traits that they could set against a pre-ordained checklist worked out by behavioural scientists. People were then selected and whittled down until there were only five left. You made the finals and so did Ellen. She was always going to be a backup for you, in case you didn't take the bait from Nico and The Taxi Driver. So not only was Ellen there as way to manipulate you, he was always there as an insurance policy. That's why you're both here. The hospital was constructed with the sole purpose of creating potential pathogen diffusing suicide bombers.

The treatments are sophisticated methods of brainwashing, that's what happens within the walls of the control room but the Finax also makes you more amenable to the brainwashing. A bit like the US LSD experiments during the 1960's. "

"You're telling me, that all the way along right from the moment that I walked into the office, they all knew what I was there for?" I asked.

"Yes, it was always the purpose of your employment. Pretty much everything that they planned for you has come to pass. You were recruited by the underground resistance. All documented by cctv and recorded ready for distribution to the media by Nemo. Unfortunately, though you're obviously thoughtful and question things. So far you've done everything they expected of you."

I shook my head. I had prided myself on questioning things, on being idealistic, but it seemed that these were the very things that they had focused on in order to recruit me in the first place. Blame the idealistic ideologue for the possible genocide. Meanwhile the company, sorts, sifts and manipulates the true information in order to hide it. But further than that, to vanish it and even people themselves, completely.

"I'm disgusted at them but I'm also disgusted at myself for falling for it." I said.

"But why?" Said Cale." How could you possibly know that this could happen? You are granting yourself powers of foresight that are pretty ridiculous. How could you know about it? You would never have been privy to anything like this in your life before. You're not a spy. You're a cleaner and that is the whole point. You were recruited to work in this job to be vanished. You are to be vanished precisely because you wouldn't have had the experience to foresee that this could happen to you. You are working for an office that is entirely invisible to most people. It has been constructed entirely for that purpose so that the average person will believe entirely the information that it puts out." Cale said.

I looked him between the eyes.

"So how do I stop it?" I said.

" You listen to me and then you go back to work in the vanishing office. Now get some sleep, I'll be back later." He said and left.

****

CHAPTER 44

Day?

I found watching the medical staff and trying to work out who was for Nemo and who was against was quite a fun new pursuit. Early morning nurse, very insistent on my taking tablets, bit authoritarian all together. For

Lunchtime nurse exchanged Finax for sugar pills. Featured in Nemo's promotional material, separated from husband and child. Hates Nemo. Against.

I had got to the stage that I could recognize the staff from behind their masks. I could deduce who they were just from their eyes. I changed my behaviour accordingly.

Afternoon nurse, speaking approvingly of Nemo when adverts were broadcast. For.

Evening nurse, Cale Reed. Against.

I found myself on tenterhooks waiting to see when Nemo's broadcast possibly featuring Ellen would take place. It hadn't taken place in the morning. I wondered how Ellen was and hoped Cale was also intending to help her. I was afraid that because she was my back up, Nemo and Stella would be ramping up preparations for using her.

Then the TV blinked on. It was one of Nemo's adverts. The central message considered the rehab centres. He was featured at the beginning, sneering as usual. Then footage of Ellen was cut in. She seemed catatonic. She looked terrible, sat perfectly still and drooling slightly. This was then interspersed with images of finax and then there were final images of Ellen sitting up quietly eating. To any person who didn't know her, this may have seemed like a miraculous recovery but this wasn't the Ellen I knew. She was like an automaton herself. I could almost see the brainwashing as it was happening. There seemed like there was no life at all behind the eyes. There was some strap line at the end of the ad calling Finax some sort of wonder drug and then the TV flashed off.

The ad was disturbing enough but I suspected that that wasn't the end of it. Then there was a tap at the door. I got out of bed and opened it and who was stood there but Ellen herself.

****

I asked her in and sat on the bed. She sat on one of the chairs next to my bed and I looked at her. She was both well dressed and tidy but she still seemed dead behind the eyes. So, the Finax was doing its job.

"How are you?" I asked.

" Ok." She said " Better, not so angry anymore. I'm ready to go home."

" Me too." I said.

" Have you seen the occupational therapist yet?" She asked.

" I didn't even know there was one." I said." No why?"

" They've found me a job working as a courier working for the same office as you do. It's part of my treatment." She said.

I bet it is. I thought.

"They thought that we could work together." She said.

"But I already have a job there as a cleaner. I don't need another job." I said.

" They suggested to me that we could make more money together if we acted as couriers. All we have to do is deliver parcels around the city. £2,000 for a couple of days work a week. I could afford to do my bar exam after a few months." She said.

So that was it, I thought. They want us both to deliver parcels around the city. Pathogen parcels. What a bunch of bastards.

However, unlike Cale had thought, they seemed to want us both to do it. He was right though that they were using Ellen to get to me but instead of using her suffering, they were going to use our friendship and sense of togetherness to get me to do what they wanted. I hated them more than before because they wanted to use and smear us both. Ellen had done nothing to deserve this. She was merely ordinary like me.

I pulled a face and said.

"I'll think about it."

Ellen grabbed and hugged me

"It'll be so fun us working together. I can't wait " She said.

"I haven't said. I'll do it yet." I warned.

"But you will though." She said. " Won't you?"

****

CHAPTER 45

I couldn't ever remember there being such a dark night. It was pitch black throughout the hospital and terribly, unnervingly silent. There didn't appear to be many, if any staff around working. It was normally, possible, even during the dead of night to hear the squeaky wheels of the gurneys and beds trundling up and down the corridor. But there was none of that.

The TV turned on and there was Stella's face against a black background. Her silver visage burned itself into my retina like a dark sun and every time I closed my eyes, I saw it there sneering at me. It was as if Nemo and Stella combined into one black hole of horror.

"You know what it is that you must do." She said, her voice seeming colder and more metallic than ever before.

"You must take the job. You must work together with Ellen. You miss her."

Subtle, I thought. Stella's not as good as she thinks she is at hypnosis. I wondered if her and Nemo had any idea at all that I was no longer taking much finax or that there was a number of medical staff, who had no intention of being loyal to them.

"Listen to Ellen." Said Stella "You can help us; you can help her. You can receive more money."

I had to stop myself from shouting at the screen. My word, all she was missing was the swinging pendulum and the swirling patterns in her eyes. This continued for around 10 minutes and then the screen flicked off again. I noticed that the purple light was filtering under the door and the low alarm was starting up again. This was my chance to try to get into the control room and make a record of what was going on. I had a terrible feeling that I would find Ellen in there, restrained on a gurney and impassive. I was worried that I would see her soul drained away by the Finax and whatever other treatments she was being forced to have. I opened the door and tried to move quickly and quietly between the pockets of light. As I moved closer to the control room, I noticed that once again there were five doors either side of the corridor and the floor, ceiling and walls were a brilliant white. I felt footsteps behind me and a male voice hissed,

"What are you doing?"

I froze and heard the footsteps moving closer and closer. I spun around and looked into the eyes of Cale Reed.

"I said what are you doing? You're not safe here." He said.

"I wanted to video what they're doing to Ellen. On my phone. To use as evidence, later. To send with the documents." I said.

"You won't be able to get in there. There's another nurse at the door. Give me your phone and I'll film it. I can hide it in my top pocket. Now go back to your room and wait there until the alarm stops and the purple light disappears." He said.

I felt a bit reluctant but everything Cale had warned me about so far had come to pass. He was the only person with the exception of Ellen that I actually felt was genuinely trustworthy. So, I put my phone in his hand and quickly walked back into my room and closed the door.

****

The low alarm and purple light continued for some time. I was very worried about Ellen and yet hopeful that Cale was there so a little part of me felt comforted that she wasn't entirely alone and friendless in the control room.

Still the waiting felt endless and it was all I could do from leaping out of bed and running down the corridor and bursting through the door however foolish or dangerous that may have been.

I must've dozed off because I woke up with a start to a gentle tapping on the door.

"Who is it?" I asked.

"It's Cale. Let me in. I've got your phone." He said.

I got up and went over to the door. I rushed into the room and locked the door.

"Did you manage to film anything?" I asked.

"Yes." He said" But I think the other nurse was a bit suspicious. I noticed that they kept looking at my pocket and asked me why I'd taken so long. I checked to see if I was followed and don't think I was but nevertheless you need to keep the phone somewhere safe."

He held out the phone in his hand and I took it from him and hid it in my bra. He smiled slightly.

"Now I'm going to need to climb out of your window just in case someone was behind me." He said.

"Good job, we're on the ground floor." I said.

"Make sure that you're calm whatever happens." He said " They still think you're in the process of being brain washed through the TV and taking the Finax. Go along with it as much as you can but keep me in touch with what's happening because when they get to the serious part of planning their mission for you, we can compose our counter plan. As yet we still don't know where they're planning to send you with the parcel bombs."

I nodded silently.

"Does Ellen know at all what they're trying to do?" I asked.

"No. Not a clue, unfortunately." Said Cale. " But don't tell her either. I know that that will be incredibly difficult for you when you know what Stella and Nemo have planned but it's really important that she doesn't panic. We don't want them to suspect that their plans have been rumbled because it will give them the opportunity to try to devise another plan and they also may try to kill you anyway and we don't want that."

"No we don't. " I said quietly. " Don't worry. I won't say anything. I'm not sure that between the Finax and the treatments that she'd believe me any way if I did."

"Probably not." He said "I'll see you soon."

He opened the curtain and then the window after it. He climbed through it swiftly and then closed the window behind him and all was quiet once again. I wondered how many people had become unknowingly embroiled in the same situation as Ellen and I had.

It was so strange and I felt that I could never view any incident in the same way ever again. Was it genuinely a terrorist act or was it some poor unsuspecting dupe recruited unawares by Nemo and co in order to carry out their dirty work for them? I was sure that I would never truly know but there was always now within me an element of doubt in the veracity of stories that I had either watched or read. It made the world seem a very uncertain place. It felt so somehow softer under foot. I almost marveled at how successful that the vanishing office had been. They had managed to dent my sense of what was real or unreal.

I was very glad that Cale and Jane were around. It felt less lonely to know that there were others who knew what was going on and also wanted to do all they could to prevent it. Yet I had never felt less important. I had been recruited solely to be a mere conduit for his views and ideas. Without my permission. My humanity was insignificant. My life itself was nothing. I couldn't even openly protest against it because as far as he was concerned, I didn't even deserve a say in my own life. I was a mere lab rat. But I was not prepared to be eradicated without my consent, either physically or emotionally. I was ready to fight back

****

CHAPTER 46

When I woke up the next morning, both Nico and The Taxi Driver were sat around my bed. I rolled my eyes a bit. If it isn't one kind of brain washing it's another. I was tempted to call their bluff about Ellen and all their bullshit about how I'd imagined her but I remembered Cale's advice about playing along and so I didn't. I just smiled and nodded as they spouted their nonsense more or less continuously for around an hour. I was so determined that they would be brought down, like Nemo. Maybe even more so because they had entirely betrayed my trust in so many ways. It was more painful, because I had at least liked The Taxi Driver, even if I'd always had a bad feeling about Nico.

"You seem to be coping much better " Nico said.

"Yes, I'm ok thanks." I answered.

"The medical staff were saying that you're going to be starting a different job when you come out, as part of your rehab." She said.

"Well yes apparently so." I said "With an old friend."

"Anyone we know?" Asked Nico.

"No, I don't think so." I said, thinking I wouldn't give her the satisfaction of trying to trip me up over Ellen.

"Well, I'm glad you stopped all that nonsense with Ellen." She said.

"The treatment is obviously really good here." I said through gritted teeth.

I looked at both Nico and The Taxi Driver carefully and wondered how they could do it and live with themselves. To lie and attempt to gaslight me in such a way. Especially when they knew what the end result was going to be. It took a severe lack of compassion to be able to tell a person that you were their long-lost family in order to manipulate them into knowingly blowing themselves up to experiment upon hundreds, maybe thousands of people also unknowingly. You might call them psychopaths. I wondered if I was doing a good enough job of hiding it.

"We'll be back to see you tomorrow." Nico said and squeezed my hand. It was all I could do to not snatch my hand away again.

"Can't wait." I said weakly.

There was a tap on the door and two nurses appeared.

"Sorry to disturb you. We're going to have to take her away now for a bath." One said.

I noticed that it was Cale. The other was a woman, who I guessed was either Jane or the other nurse who was working to get rid of Nemo.

"Be our guest." Said The Taxi Driver.

Cale and the other nurse unhooked all of the machinery from me and wheeled me out of the room. As we left, I noticed Cale drop something on the floor behind the bin. I wondered if Nico and The Taxi Driver had noticed but they seemed so deeply involved in their conversation that they didn't seem to notice it.

We went out of the door and Cale put his finger to his lips. I was intrigued to find out where it was that they'd be taking me because as far as I was aware there were no bathing facilities within the hospital apart from the largely rubbish en suite showers in the loo at the side of the bedroom. The pushed me towards one of the lifts and then we got in. We ascended a couple of floors and then Cale pressed the emergency stop button. The lift stopped suddenly with a judder, we all jumped slightly.

"I'm not going for a bath, am I? " I said

"Well deduced." Said Cale. "It was the only way we could get you out of the way for a chat. They can't spy on us in here with the emergency stop on." I nodded.

"I noticed that you dropped something behind the bin. What was it?" I asked.

"Yes, I thought you'd noticed. You're an eagle eye, aren't you?" Cale said. " Yes, you're right, I did. It was a mini recorder. To see if we can pick something up from Nico while we're stuck in here. She might decide to have a chat with The Taxi Driver while we're not around. I don't think they noticed."

I nodded in agreement.

"Anyway, let me introduce Jane." Cale said. " As you know she'll be helping us disrupt Nemo's plans for you and Ellen. Slowly but surely, she's weaning Ellen off the Finax. We can't stop her from having the other treatments at the moment but cutting down the drugs will definitely help."

"Hi." Jane said and shook my hand. It was strange finally meeting Jane after all I'd heard about her from Nico and The Taxi Driver.

"Would I be right in thinking that everything that The Taxi Driver and Stella told me about you was totally untrue?" I asked.

"Almost everything." She said "He isn't my Dad and Nico isn't my sister either but it was totally true that they tried to concoct a story about me being found with a needle in my arm and also smearing me as a drug smuggler but I'm sure that Cale told you that." I nodded.

"We need to find out where you and Ellen are going to be sent on your delivery and also what pathogen they are wanting you to disseminate. somehow, we need to hack into the Nemo and Co system to be able to get that information. It is very likely that Stella and Nemo will want to speak to you about changing jobs. They've tried to get to you through Ellen and as far as they know, they've been successful. They're not likely to tell you much before they send you on your mission. They want to keep you in the dark as much as possible. They don't want you to know what's happening before time. Now unfortunately we don't have anyone inside the office at the moment. We're likely going to have to hack in remotely and there's a possibility that we won't manage to do that before they send you out with the packages. We don't know if they'll detonate them the first time out or they will send you out a few times first. We need a plan for you to be put in case it's the former. " Jane said.

"My God, it's pretty high stakes all of this, isn't it?" I said.

"Pretty much." Cale replied.

"Is it at all possible that we'll be killed and smeared whatever we do?" I asked.

"Yes, it is, but we're going to do our damndest to make sure that that doesn't happen. Unlike Nemo's puppet resistance, we do actually have a number of people who know what they're doing and who will be able to help. It's just that you and Ellen have got to play an important part in it. Then Nemo and Stella won't know that they're beaten until they actually are." Cale said.

I took a deep breath and for about the thousandth time, wondered how on earth I found myself in a situation like this.

"So, do you have a backup plan?" I asked.

"Yes." Cale said.

"We do have links with a construction company. They have been digging trenches within a five-mile radius of a list of possible targets under the guise of building works, road resurfacing. You name it. If you receive the packages, we would ask you to deliver them safely to one of the trenches and then they will dispose of them safely. At the moment the only problem is not knowing which delivery will feature the pathogens. We're hoping that Nico and The Taxi Driver will be indiscreet enough to discuss it while we're out of the room. We can't guarantee they will but maybe they'll be foolish enough to give us something." He said.

"We can but hope." I said.

I really hated the thought that I might be carrying around Nemo's plague deliveries. For my own sake as well as other people's.

"Yes, well hopefully we'll know something more soon." Cale said. "I think we'd better go back before anyone gets suspicious. "

And with that he hit the emergency button again and the lift started moving upwards. Once we got to the top of the building the doors opened and there was a porter waiting to come into it. I recognized him from before when I'd tried to enter the control room. He gave us all a funny look but said nothing. I thought that it was likely that he was loyal to Nemo and wondered if he had any idea that we were plotting against the organization. It was hard to tell. Nobody really gave anything away whatever side you were on.

****

CHAPTER 47

Soon enough we were back down in the hospital room. The Taxi Driver and Nico were still there and were talking away amongst themselves. Cale nodded at me as if to say pick up the tape recorder once they'd gone and then himself and Jane left the room. Nico and The Taxi Driver didn't really say anything to else to me other than small talk. They both kissed my cheek and left. I was reminded of Judas and wondered how many pieces of silver they'd got and if it was worth it.

I gave it a few minutes to make sure that they had actually left and then I searched behind the bin to pick up the recorder that Cale had dropped behind the bin. I was very tempted to listen to it, but thought that it was likely to be too risky. So, I decided to store it in the other cup of my bra until Cale appeared again.

****

I hadn't seen Ellen for a few days either in the garden or as a visitor. It just felt too quiet. There were no adverts or programmes playing on the TV and neither Nico or The Taxi Driver had visited. It was the calm before the storm.

I was extremely apprehensive about what form Cale's plan would take. Not because I didn't trust him or Jane. I did but I couldn't see how they'd be able to discover when Ellen and I would be delivering the pathogen packages. Stella could decide to change the plan at the last minute and so always leaving us with very limited options. Would we be able to get rid of the packages safely? After all, none of us knew what kind of pathogens the packages would contain. Would it be a virus or a nerve agent? Different pathogens would require different responses. I was very afraid of Nemo succeeding mainly because of the destruction he was planning but more than that, I didn't want my life to be invented or rewritten especially when I had actively been trying to work against that very outcome.

I continued to write my code word records thinking that I must make sure that I provided a key somewhere safe, then if anything ended up going wrong, I'd at least have some record that would dispel any propaganda that might making its way out of the vanishing office.

Most of the day had passed and neither Cale nor Jane had visited my room to bring my fake medicine. I was becoming slightly nervous that they had been found out. The encounter with the porter in the lift had been wordless and yet a slightly fraught one. If they had been discovered and been reported it was likely that I'd be none the wiser.

****

CHAPTER 48

By lights out, I was getting really anxious but just before I dropped off to sleep there was a familiar knock at the door. It was Cale. He was carrying a notebook.

" Are you ready to hear if there's anything on the recorder?" He wrote in the book.

"Isn't it a bit risky?" I wrote back.

"It is but you deserve to hear it. You and Ellen are taking the greatest risks with the packages. So only right that you should hear." He wrote.

"But what if they have bugs in here?" I wrote.

"They do but they're located in the TV so if it's broken or un-plugged, they won't hear anything." He wrote back. He then un-plugged the TV.

It seemed extremely lax on their part.

"Remember they still think you're taking the Finax ." He said. "They can't fathom that anyone could actually outsmart them and so because of that there are lots of gaps and opportunities in the methods they use to try to control things. They're unable to conceive that it's possible that anyone is as clever as they are and because of that it makes them sloppy."

I simply nodded. To be on the safe side in case there were any bugs that Cale hadn't encountered, I put on the radio that was part of my phone and left it on my bed, next to the light. Cale and I took the recorder into the bathroom and turned the shower on. He then pulled out some ear buds from his pocket and put one in my ear then the other one into his own. He locked the bathroom door and pressed play.

It was slightly crackly at first. The topic of conversation was how much better they both thought I was doing. This carried on for about a minute and then there was a loud shushing sound. Then there was silence for a few moments and Nico spoke.

"It's alright, they've definitely gone."

"Do we know any more?" The Taxi Driver asked.

"Not really, they haven't made the final decision yet, but it will be both of them. They've already got the write up ready to give to the media. It's very well done. They're also going to doctor some dashcam footage." Nico said.

"Bastards." I wrote and then, "They obviously are that stupid."

Cale simply nodded and continued to listen.

"Stella has made it known that there's an antidote on hand for significant persons or for those who would be unduly mourned by the public. Too many elderly people or children etc. A few don't matter but we have to keep those numbers down."

I could only shake my head at this. I was so livid.

"Have they decided what they're going to use yet?" The Taxi Driver asked.

"No not completely." Nico answered.

"Possibly the virus they've been testing here but it doesn't seem to be especially virulent. So that's unlikely. Possibly a flu variant but they haven't totally ruled out chemicals."

The Taxi Driver cleared his throat.

"Are they sure that the women will do it?" He said.

"They've both been here a month now. Pumped full of Finax and those mind reprogramming interventions. Stella is constantly projected into their rooms as well. I'm fairly sure that they are both so brainwashed now that they don't know which way is up or down." Nico said.

"What a cow!" I mouthed. I was glad be proving Nico wrong.

I was neither brainwashed nor the stupid idiot that she obviously thought I was. Her smug coldness infuriated me. But it was her hypocritical psychopathy that was worse. Pretending to be a freedom fighter against the authoritarian Nemo and Co when she was working with them hand in glove.

"When will we find out anything new?" The Taxi Driver said.

"I don't know at the moment. It could be today. It could be a week from now. It just depends on the conditions being right. Stella is going to perform a test on the subjects in the next couple of days. That then gives us enough time to see if they're ready to perform their mission or not. She should be able to work out if they can withstand the rigours ahead."

"What does that mean? " I mouthed.

Cale just shrugged. A couple of days meant that Ellen and I were likely to be tested tomorrow in some as yet unknown way. That meant hardly any time to be mentally prepared for it.

"Anyway, it's about half an hour since they took her away, they could be back any minute." Said Nico.

"OK we'd better start discussing other things then." Said The Taxi Driver." Do you think she knows that we lied to her and that we're really working for the other side?"

"Unlikely." Said Nico." I don't think she has the brains."

The blood pumping through my veins felt almost white with the fury. I was buzzing with rage. Cale could see how angry I was and so turned off the recording. I wasn't sure if I able to keep my cool the next time I saw Nico. I felt like I could tear her into a thousand pieces. Then out of nowhere there was a knock at the door.

"Staff nurse Harrison, are you in there?" A voice called out.

"Yes. "Cale answered." I'm just helping the patient wash her hair. " He nodded to the shower which was still running. I got in and pulled the curtain across.

" Well, when you're done, can you come down and give Dr Freeman a hand because he's having difficulty with a patient?" The voice said.

"Yes, won't be long." He said and then put his ear to the door.

"It's ok. He's gone." Cale said.

"That was close." I said.

"Yes, too close. I think we're going to have to watch out for Hargreaves. I've a feeling that he might be Lawson's replacement." Cale said.

"Hargreaves?" I asked.

"The porter from earlier. If he starts snooping around in here just be really careful. I don't trust him." Cale said.

"Yes, I know what you mean." I said and turned the shower off and stepped into my dressing gown. Cale then unlocked the door and I got into bed and as I did so, he said.

"Keep your eyes peeled and be ready for anything." Then he left and closed the door behind him.

I wondered what tests Stella had planned for us. It made me shiver just thinking about it.

****

I decided that I needed to go for a walk in the garden as early as possible the next day. I wasn't sure what I would find as I left the confines of my room. The environment changed so totally and so often, that I was ready for anything. In fact, when I entered the corridor and it was exactly the same as the last time, I'd seen it, I was almost disappointed. The garden was empty there was no sign of either staff or other patients there. It was as if everyone had just totally disappeared. I could smell the trees and flowers and they still seemed to be, the real living plants that had appeared after the last change and not the plastic facsimiles that had populated the garden before.

Then out of the corner of my eye, I noticed a very tall metallic figure. It was Stella. She moved silently towards me and sat down. I supposed that I was about to be tested but what form that would take, I had no idea.

"How did you know that I'd be here?" I asked.

"You're a creature of habit like most humans." She said " You come here most days and then you fill in your crossword puzzle books."

"That's true " I replied "So what is it that you wanted to talk to me about?"

"Your progress here." Stella said. " You've improved enormously thanks to the treatment programme of drugs and therapy."

"Well, I do feel better." I said.

"That's good." She said. " Now someone approached you about starting a different job for us, didn't they?"

"Yes, they did." I answered.

"Who was it?" Stella asked.

I had the indispensable feeling that she was trying to catch me out.

"One of the other patients." I said. "I don't remember her name but I do recognize her."

"Hmmmm." Stella said." Yes, that's right. Don't worry about re-membering who they are. That's a side effect of the drugs, am-nesia, I mean but it goes in time and it's a price worth paying for the delusions going away. "

I just nodded unsure of what to say.

"So, do you think you'll be happy doing this other work for us? Delivering important packages?" She asked.

"Well, it'll be a change " I said." Do I have to get up quite so early?"

Stella chuckled.

"No, no, no, that's not necessary. This is strictly a nine to five job. The money is better." She said.

"Yes, I know. They told me " I said, amazed that so far I'd managed to avoid saying Ellen's name.

"It will help aid both of your recoveries and you both working together will be helpful to the company and our clients. These are very important and precious packages so it's very important that you both take them exactly where we tell you to." She said.

She looked at me closely and intently for a moment.

"We know exactly where they should be going. We will fit each package with a tracking device so we'll be totally aware where each package is on every step of its journey."

I looked at Stella and tried to remain impassive. I couldn't help feeling that it was absolutely essential that I didn't give anything away. It was obvious that Stella was probing to see if I would give anything away. I wondered if she already suspected that I had no intention of delivering any of these packages nor be slandered as one of the culprits who visited catastrophe upon whoever was chosen to be the victims of these experiments.

"It's obviously a very important job." I said " I'm flattered that you thought of me, but I'm not entirely sue why. Surely there were other people who worked for the company for longer or who have had more experience of such things. "

"You've shown a lot of promise and you obviously work hard. I know you've got involved with those underground resistance thugs but you've moved beyond that now. You've settled in here very well and redeemed yourself so we thought you deserved a reward for your efforts." Stella said.

If I hadn't known better what Stella's plans actually were, I could've found myself believing it. I found it really frightening how persuasive she could be either through encouragement or sadism. She was extremely good at both. There was no wonder that Ellen had been convinced being pumped full of Finax and not knowing what Stella's actual agenda was. It both saddened and angered me that she had the ability to draw vulnerable people in to do her bidding and then be scapegoated. She reminded me of an enormous chrome scorpion and we were the toads she was trying to sting relentlessly.

"Do you have any idea where we'll be delivering?" I asked.

"All over the city." She said. "Mainly hospitals, probably businesses and some residential housing. Honestly it could take you anywhere. We probably won't know much until the morning you start. Why do you ask?"

I knew that I had to be careful about the about the questions I asked. She was intelligent and easily suspicious. Cale was sure that neither Stella nor Nemo knew that he was alive or that he'd been disrupting my brainwashing. I wasn't entirely convinced that they didn't know. I could conceive of a scenario where they were indeed aware but pretended otherwise to reel us in further and maybe even catch Jane and Cale and I really didn't want that to happen.

"I just want to get some idea. It's not like cleaning. You need to have a good sense of direction. Of where you are and where you're going in a delivery job." I said. " I'm not sure that I know the city as well as I need to."

"You must have confidence in yourself." Stella said. "You will be making a very important contribution and as far as knowing where you're going goes, we will be giving you both a hand-held GPS to help you find where you're going to. So, you won't be getting lost. We'll do our best to make sure that you know exactly where it is, you're going. We'll help in any way that we can. Our reputation as a business depends on it."

She then patted me on the head with her long, metal fingers. I was very unnerved by it and almost flinched. I knew that she'd could easily crush my head between her hands, if she so decided. But in some way, being gently stroked by those thin cold fingers was worse. It was like being in the slow asphyxiating grip of a boa constrictor, tightening and tightening in an almost imperceptible manner until you could no longer breathe.

J.E. CLARKSON

****

CHAPTER 49

Was that the test? The thought just continued going round and round in my head. She was definitely probing for information and yet it seemed altogether way too straightforward. I was waiting for the other shoe to drop.

I didn't see Cale or Jane again that day and Ellen apparently had disappeared again. I had an awful vision of her being hooked up to various ever more invasive machines, as Stella found more and more diabolical ways to strip her of her original personality. Even though I was playing along, I was very grateful for my mental autonomy at least. I was resisting even if Stella had no clue about it.

I did shiver slightly thinking what on earth I would have done without Cale's help. It frightened me to think that I could have been like Ellen having my very soul stripped away without my knowledge. It horrified me to think that Stella not only wanted to erase us so that we'd be her pawns but also all of those lives who had been chosen to be experimented on. Without knowing it, they had already been erased, they had become no-things. They were not even considered to be human any more, they were merely subjects to be scrutinized and categorized. They were to be annihilated and once they were, their annihilation was to be documented in graphs and statistics. They were to no longer be vital, breathing individuals but merely a black typed figure on a piece of paper or a number on a laptop screen.

It dawned on me that that's what the vanishing office was, an instrument for the dehumanization of people. Its purpose was to decide the ultimate value of the lives of the test subjects. If you were deemed important enough, you would be given an antidote or not chosen at all. If you weren't, then you were ultimately invisible, valued only as a number in the pages of some study or other intended to prove or disprove some wild theory that the experiments were supposed to explore.

I then had a thought. I'd not managed to get much information out of Stella. She'd been deliberately vague apart from mentioning the GPS. I wondered if it might serve a dual purpose as both a means of giving us directions but also serving as a remote detonator. It made sense and it was exactly the kind of crafty method that Stella would use to ensure that we carried out her plans unwittingly. I knew that I must get back to my room as quickly as possible to make a note about it in my puzzle books before I forgot about it.

I made my way towards the entrance of the hospital and noticed that the porter, Stella's new thug was stood right in front of it. He appeared to be almost leering as he had a slight, sinister smile on his face.

"What are you doing here all on your own?" He said and started walking towards me.

I knew in my guts that this was dangerous. He kept on moving towards me and he said.

"I'm asking you again what are you doing all on your own?"

"I was just getting some fresh air and now I'm going back to my room." I said.

"No, I think you need to stay here with me. I can help make your life much easier if you can do me a favour now and again." He said.

As he spoke, he grabbed my wrist and held it tightly. I tried to move out of his grasp but the more I tried to wriggle free, the tighter his grip became.

" You're a feisty one." He said "Even better. I like a bit of a challenge."

Just as I thought there was no escape. I heard a familiar voice ring out.

"What the hell do you think you're doing?" It was Cale. The porter let go of my wrist and I ran towards Cale. In that moment I felt like hugging him but I didn't. I just stood very close as the porter scowled put his head down and skulked away.

"You need to watch him." Cale said.

"Yes, I gathered that." I replied.

"We need to have a chat. " He said. "But not here."

****

We walked back down the corridor to my room in silence. I kept wondering just how long I had in the hospital before I was shipped out and into the courier job. That was one of the hardest things. Being in limbo.

We reached my room. I sat on my bed and Cale sat on the chair. He took a deep breath and then let it all out in one big sigh.

" It looks like they're going to try to move you in a couple of days." He said." But we still don't know yet if they're planning to detonate the packages during your first shift or afterwards."

"Stella did come to talk to me and I did think that she might have unintentionally given me some extra information." I said.

"Oh yes " Said Cale. "What's that?"

"Well, she mentioned that Ellen and I would both be given a gps to help us find where we're supposed to be going but wouldn't it be possible that they could be used for remote detonators too? "I asked.

"Yes, I think they could. They'd also be able to erase any trace of their giving it to you, any data that they may hold with regards to you and their relationship to you." He said

"We're being hung out to dry, aren't we?" I said, not expecting an answer.

"Not by me. I hope you know." Cale said.

"No not by you. You and Jane are two of the few people I don't feel like that about." I said.

"I'm glad because we will do everything possible to prevent this catastrophe happening." He said " We need to be as prepared as possible with a backup plan in case you're moved before I can talk to you again. I think the GPS

might be the key to that. We could use them to distract Nemo and make sure they go in one direction and the packages in another, namely into one of the ditches. We may need to arrange for a couple of replacement couriers to move the packages while you and Ellen keep hold of the gps and take them to wherever the packages are supposed to be going. I'll arrange for them today while you're still here. They won't have good enough cctv surveillance to know that it isn't you and Ellen. We'll also make sure of that."

"How?" I asked

"Just trust me. I was disrupting Nemo and Co. almost from the beginning. I've got ways and means. I'm not going to tell you too much so that they can't try to get it out of you if you're rumbled before time." Cale said.

"Well, that's reassuring." I said.

I sat there quietly mulling over the enormity of what lay ahead. To be the vehicle of a possible biological or chemical weapons attack was terrifying especially when there was so much uncertainty around when it might happen. I did trust Cale but even slightly stepping into such a dangerous scenario was pretty frightening. I felt I needed a definite way to extricate myself and Ellen were we to find ourselves holding the parcels.

"I'm very tempted to just refuse to do it. I'm disgusted they're going to do this and they've chosen us to do it." I said.

"I can understand that." Cale said and put a reassuring hand on my shoulder.

"It's totally unfair and that they want to use you in this way is appalling. Unfortunately, though if you do refuse to do it it's likely that they'll kill you both anyway and still detonate the bomb afterwards. They'd still write what they like about you, which is also totally unfair. So, I think that despite the holes in our counter plans, it's still the best way to keep you both alive and to take down, Nemo and Stella. Do you trust me?" He asked.

He looked at me intensely. I nodded reluctantly. What he said made sense. I'd already seen that Nemo could kill you off both literally and in print. He had made sure to pick two ordinary people to help bring his plans to fruition. People like Ellen and I were invisible to most people. Our lives a copy of so many others. He saw us as a couple of stupid losers, people who'd made wrong decisions, who were easy to dismiss and as such, expendable. But I was determined I wouldn't allow him to write off our lives so easily.

"Cale, I promise you; I am determined to do anything to bring this charlatan and his company down. Nemo, Stella, Nico and The Taxi Driver, the whole damn lot of them. I'm afraid, very afraid that something will go wrong but all I ask is that if it does, that you will make sure that the truth is out there for everyone to see. I want people like us, ordinary people to know all about it. Every detail, so they know what the plans were and how they could have been chosen as Guinea pigs themselves. Please don't let it be written away or hidden. I don't want people to think that it was my idea but more importantly, I want them to see that people wanted to make the lives of those who were experimented on unimportant and only because they were ordinary, like us. Please don't allow them to do that." I said.

Cale nodded and when he spoke his voice broke.

"I promise."

****

CHAPTER 50

Possibly waiting for death makes you think. It colours every-thing you do. It isn't universally negative either. Very ordinary things take on a new feeling of intensity and you drink in every moment. This could be your last night's sleep in a comfy bed or a last cup of coffee. The negative side of it though is a bit like having a ten tonne weight suspended above your head ready to fall down and crush you but you just never quite know when.

I did sometimes feel like the grim reaper might be sat on the edge of my bed. I fully expected to see them there but the weird thing was that were I to pull their hood, I didn't expect to see a skull underneath it, I was fully prepared for Stella's chrome face to be peering out and the scythe in her hand to be replaced with a detonator.

But grim reaper fantasies aside, possible imminent death some-how boosted my courage. I definitely didn't want to die of course and certainly not in the way Nemo and Stella had planned for me, but suddenly all the peripheral stuff was falling away. It became less significant and I was calmer somehow and less anxious. I wondered at first if those medical staff loyal to Nemo were still somehow secreting Finax into my system but I didn't see how they could be. Cale and Jane seemed like the only medical staff who nursed me now. So, it seemed that the calm was genuine and not chemical at all. So those last few days in the hospital were quite tranquil. There were no more fake visits from Nico or The Taxi Driver to frustrate me and I was even starting to become quite fond of the garden.

Then one morning the porter and Cale arrived in my room wheeling a suitcase.

"To pack your stuff in." The porter said and then left.

"Today's the day." I said and raised an eyebrow.

"You ready?" Said Cale

"No." I said and laughed.

"I've managed to sneak a burner phone in to the inside zip pocket of the suit case. Stella's new surveillance man isn't as thorough as he thinks he is. Now Nico and The Taxi Driver are going to appear to drive you home so keep your wits about you. They may try to ask you questions." Cale said.

"Don't worry I'm not going to give anything away. They annoy me as much if not more so than Stella and Nemo do. I won't be telling them anything." I said.

"Good. I'll send as much information on the packages as I can, when I can. We've got into the system but haven't decoded the information yet. Just try to keep your eyes open." Cale said.

"I will." I replied and then moved forward to give Cale a hug. He seemed taken aback at first but then I whispered in his ear.

"Take my puzzle books and other phone. They're stuck in the bottom pillowcase on the bed. All the records I've been keeping are in there. There's a key to all of code words in my phone and the words are in the puzzle books. They're a record of everything I've seen here and in Nemo and Co. right from the beginning. Make sure you keep it somewhere safe and pass it on to someone who will make it a matter of public record. Especially if I don't survive."

"You will survive." Cale said. "But I promise I'll do whatever you ask."

As I pulled away, I saw The Taxi Driver and Nico stood in the doorway. I wasn't sure if they were smiling or grimacing.

****

CHAPTER 51

The drive home was very strange. The atmosphere swung from eerie silence to overly jolly. It was like they were both trying too hard. They didn't seem to realize that I had worked it out. I did feel extremely odd being in the company of these two people who were pretending so hard to be my family. Because I was so angry at their betrayal it almost served as a shield. I could hold them at arm's length and pretend that it was down to the Finax or just because I was tired. I looked out on the city from the taxi window and marvelled at how different It felt compared to the last time I'd travelled in there. All of that sense of comfort and familiarity had gone, blown away by all of the lies and plotting

The city itself now appeared grey and flat. We drove past the hospital and thought about mentioning it but reminded myself that they had tried to convince me that I had imagined it all and that I was delusional, so I didn't bother. But the thing was I could plainly see dark stains on the ground where Lawson had obviously landed and there were also dark tyre treads where the ambulance had speeded up and hit the security guard. There was no denying it. There was physical evidence. But I didn't need to say anything. I knew what had really happened and that was all that mattered now.

****

I was concerned that they would want me to stay with them or that they might want to come into the flat and carry on the charade a bit longer. Thankfully they didn't and they almost looked relieved as they dropped me off.

As I opened the flat door, I took a look around but took it as read that that my flat would now be bugged. Stella would want to make sure that she kept as close an eye upon me as possible so aside from ordering a takeaway and sitting in bed, I made my mind up to be as careful as possible about what I did from that moment onwards.

I sat in bed munching happily on a Chinese banquet. It somehow tasted better just sitting there eating it in my own bed. I'd almost expected that the hospital porter would be the one delivering it but Stella was unlikely to be using the same operatives outside the hospital as those inside. As I sat there eating and catching up with the news, my phoned trilled into life. It was a message from Stella. At first, I was confused, wondering how on earth she could've got the number but then another message followed from Cale in quick succession.

"Forwarded this from your phone. If you don't reply she'll get suspicious. "

The second message read.

"How can I?" I answered. "The number will be different."

A few seconds later another message popped into my inbox.

"Not so." It read." We made sure that you had exactly the same number as you had before. She won't realize."

"How is that possible?" I texted back.

"I can't tell you I'm afraid. Not yet anyway. Just text her back." He replied.

Cale was obviously seriously connected and yet I was still doubtful so before I replied to Stella's original message, I needed to double check that the SIM card was identical to my original number. I took the battery out and then removed the sim and sure enough, the number was exactly the same.

I scrolled back up to open Stella's message. It read.

"Congratulations on your recovery and welcome back home.

Your new contract begins now but you don't begin deliveries for another couple of days. Rest and recuperate as far as you can and we will be in contact in the next couple of days regarding times and delivery routes. £1,000 is being paid into your account. Good to have you back. Stella."

Life is cheap. I thought as I texted back.

"Thank you."

I sat back and rested my head on the headboard. Normally I'd not enjoyed the quiet and would've done whatever I could to try to escape it but after all the loud mania of the last month, this silence was a comforting luxury. I wanted to wrap myself up in it and drift away to some fantasy land where everything was peaceful and people had benevolent motives. It was lovely to lie there and dream but unfortunately, I knew that the world was far grittier and crueller than most people had the capacity to imagine.

****

CHAPTER 52

It was completely dark. Even the street lights were off. I wondered if there had been some sort of power cut while I was asleep. Nothing electrical in the flat appeared to be working. I looked out of the window to see if I could see any clue as to why. I could hear torrential rain beating down and bouncing off the pavement and yet it was so dark outside that I could only hear it. I couldn't see it all.

A cold breeze seemed to emanate through the window and other unseen gaps. It almost seemed as if a pale blue dust was hovering over everything. It was the only thing that punctuated through the darkness and it appeared to roll through in waves. I wondered if it was a kind of poison sent to silently contaminate us all. It wouldn't have surprised me. It had Stella written all over it. A silent assassin in the night just like one of the Biblical plagues but there were no daubs on the door to protect anyone.

The only thing that made me question these wild thoughts was the fact that Nemo and Co. really wanted a scapegoat to carry the can so I just discounted it. I continued to look out of the window hoping to get some idea of what was going on. I could see a number of lights equally distanced apart, seemingly moving in straight lines. I squinted and crouched down low so that I could watch what was going on and remain unseen.

The lights just carried on moving closer and closer. Then I noticed that a few of them changed formation and moved into a more random pattern. I realized that it was rows of people carrying torches and they seemed to be looking up and down the street and in some cases stopping at the doors of buildings and then disappearing. In spite of the great numbers of people, there was absolute silence. They didn't make a sound. I carried on watching and slowly a vague sense of horror came over me.

I realized that they were taking people out of their houses. Some people walked and others were prone and so they were carried out. It wasn't every house. Only certain buildings were chosen. I then noticed that the people who'd been rounded up had been moved into waiting cars. This also happened silently and with no visible protest. God only knows where they were going. I ran to my bag and grabbed the burner phone and set the video camera to record. I needed to make sure that I had more evidence to send to Cale as I was in absolutely no doubt now that this was down to Stella.

As I continued to film, I noticed that more and more people were being removed from their homes and put into vehicles. It seemed that there only around five properties that were left alone. The vehicles drove off with only very dim headlights lighting the road in front of them. Then it was entirely dark and quiet again for a few moments. Then as if the power cut had been reversed, all of the electronics came back on again. I looked back out of the window and saw that the streetlights had come on. I could also see a patchwork of lights emanating from the other flats. I wondered how many of them were now uninhabited either for the short term or for good. I felt I needed to send Cale a message about what I'd just witnessed and also sent a very short video clip to show him what was happening. I rewatched it before sending it and blinked in disbelief. I'd seen it but my brain was rebelling. It couldn't be true. I didn't want it to be true. I knew it wasn't a happy fate that was to befall all of those people.

I sent off the message and then decided to make myself a coffee. I knew that it would be virtually impossible to sleep for the rest of the night now after what I'd just seen. I then went into the kitchen and idly looked out as I waited for the coffee to boil. I thought I saw a glimmer of something metallic out of the corner of my eye and so I followed the gleam until I saw Stella standing there under one of the street lamps. She stood there stock still for a moment. It seemed as though she was looking right at me. I was sure that she wanted me to know for certain that she was behind the unholy spectacle that I had just witnessed. She carried on just standing there as if to say:

"You can believe your eyes. But what are you going to do about it?"

Then she smiled the slightest of smiles and moved out of the light and all I could see was the faintest glimmer of chrome speeding through the darkness like a laser.

I felt totally hopeless for a while seeing this possible erasure of almost an entire street. What next? A borough? A city? A country? What made up the criteria for removal?

But then the dark night brightened to a vivid blue as it does a few minutes before the sun starts to come up. I heard the plaintive song of the morning birds and realized that I must steel myself to my purpose for the sake of those I had just witness disappear. I had to ensure that those who were being taken away would not disappear into the night with no witnesses. I would be the witness and would make sure that whatever happened to me that the whole world knew about it.

****

I learned a hard lesson the next morning. I turned on the TV, hoping, even expecting that the vanishing of so many people would be the top story on the news. But there was nothing. Complete radio silence. Then the brutal realization hit me that this sort of thing could be constantly happening under a cloud of secrecy. Was the media deliberately covering it up or just choosing not to report it? Were neighbours in the area keeping quiet or just refusing to get involved? It was likely that there were many layers to any conspiracy of silence. All of it shocked me to the core.

We all think that that sort of thing doesn't happen to us or to those we know. It happens to others either in a different place or time. That's the biggest lie we tell ourselves. It can't happen to me. But of course, it can and it does, because as much as we hate to realize it, we are those other people.

As I replayed last night's events through my head for the umpteenth time, I wondered what on earth it was that sentenced all of those people to their fate. They couldn't all be rebels. Maybe in their arrogance, Stella and Nemo believed that they wouldn't be missed or that if they were no one would have the power or incentive to do anything about it. But surely, I wasn't the only witness. Surely friends and family would wonder where their loved ones had gone.

I looked out of the window and there was no one on the street. Not one person. No dog walkers. No window shoppers. Not even any cyclists making their way to work. It was totally deserted. My burner phone beeped. It was a message from Cale.

"Got your message and saved the file. My spies tell me that this happened all over the city. There's no official recognition. My guess is that it is happening everywhere. Be very careful. They've left you alone for now because of what they're going to try to do but I'm sure they will be keeping a very close eye on you."

I had no doubt about that. Seeing Stella standing under the street light had felt like a provocation. I sensed that they knew that I was hellbent on disrupting their plans and they just wanted to see what I would do. Whether I would incriminate myself somehow and make their job easier. I decided to keep well out of the way to prevent that from happening. Even if it meant staying in for the next few days.

I turned the TV on and after a few minutes watching, I couldn't get over how much it was like the hospital TV. There seemed to be a lot more adverts and programmes featuring Nemo and there was even a couple of adverts for Finax, which is something that I'd not noticed before I went into the hospital. A bit of me wondered if like within the hospital, Nemo and Co. had now decided they wanted to take their brainwashing programme a little bit further. It seemed like the hospital had been in preparation for other things.

****

CHAPTER 53

By lunchtime, I realized that I couldn't stay in any longer. I was going stir crazy just alone with my thoughts. I pulled on a coat and went for a walk. I put a phone in my pocket thinking that I wanted to make a document of everything I saw.

When I walked outside of the front door, I realized that I didn't recognize anything at all. It all looked entirely different. The lamppost seemed singed and rusted, the clear outer glass appeared to be blackened from the inside as if the bulbs had exploded and caught fire. As I walked around the block, I saw the same pattern over and over again. Burned out windows, blackened benches and broken street lamps. There was no sign of life anywhere. The shops were closed and appeared damaged.

I took out my phone and started to film. It was as if a great fire had ripped through the area. Everything was twisted, burnt or broken. It was a vision of Armageddon. It was very puzzling though as I hadn't seen the source of this destruction from the night before. I couldn't have missed it or slept through it for the damage was too vast.

I turned a corner and saw a lone figure sat on a bench. As I drew closer, I realized that it was Ellen. She was just sat there, holding a plastic bag in her left hand. She looked completely spaced out and I was unsure if she would recognize me at all.

"Ellen?" I said. " What are you doing here?"

"I got a message about delivering an envelope here. They even gave me a lift but the address doesn't seem to exist. I had a parcel for a primary school and another one for a hospital. Didn't they ring you?" She asked.

All of the colour drained from my face as I now knew why Stella had been standing under the lamppost looking incredibly smug.

"Shit.Shit.Shit." I said.

****

CHAPTER 54

"Ellen put the parcel down under the bench and move away from it. As quick as you can. Come on." I shouted.

It didn't seem to compute. She was struggling to comprehend what I was saying.

"Ellen!" I said sharply. "Wake up and put it down."

She just sat there catatonic. I noticed that there was an old metal dustbin about twenty metres away and I grabbed the parcel out of her hand. I ran to the bin, put the bag inside and then put the lid on secured by a brick. Ellen continued to just sit there impassively. So, I grabbed her hand and pulled her as I ran. She just followed on behind, floppy like a rag doll. I had no idea how long we had before the package exploded but I knew I had to do two things urgently, find some shelter and ring Cale to let him know what was happening.

I grabbed my phone and pressed speed dial. I prayed that he would pick up straight away. It rang and rang and then went straight to voicemail.

"Brilliant." I thought but left a message.

"Cale. It's happening now. In my neighbourhood. I've left the parcel in a dustbin. I don't know how long we've got."

I heaved and gasped with the effort of trying to talk and run at the same time. I could see that my flat was only a few metres away and just before we managed to get there a black people carrier screeched in front of us and cut off our path. We had no means of getting round it. My heart sank through the floor as I felt we'd been outmanoeuvred at every turn. I fully expected the door to open and for Stella to get out and start laughing at us. That, or a number of black clad paramilitaries piling out and sticking their gun muzzles against the sides of our heads.

But no, something amazing happened. When the door opened, it was Cale and Jane inside.

"Get in." He hissed." We've got about ten minutes to get out of here."

"Where are we going?" I asked.

"My safe house." Said Jane. "If we put our foot down, we can be out of the city before it explodes. To warn you that there are already reports about an incident. They haven't linked either of you to it yet, but they will do, as you know so you need to come away with us for a while."

I looked at Ellen. She was still expressionless. She hadn't really comprehended anything that had just happened.

"Are you able to leave everything behind?" Cale asked me.

"I don't really have anything now do I? In about an hour the whole world will think I'm a dead terrorist so it's the only option I have isn't it?" I said.

"Pretty much." Said Cale. " But don't be too despondent. There are advantages to being dead."

I looked at Ellen and then back at him and Jane and nodded. This was the nearest thing I had to family and if I was going to go anywhere, I may as well go with them. I sank down low in my seat as Cale accelerated and then as we drove out of the city limits, I was sure I could hear a sound extremely similar to the low vibration alarm and as I looked through the rear-view mirror, I could see a familiar purple light diffusing across the landscape. Cale's eyes met mine through the mirror and he turned the radio on without saying a word.

"And now we have more on the terrorist incident in the eastern part of the city." The radio presenter droned." Entire streets have been wiped out in a haze of burning particles, the like of which we've never seen before. We are going over live to our crime correspondent, Nico Tucker."

"And so, it begins." Said Cale.

I couldn't say anything in reply. I could only look at the mirrored sky scrapers and notice that the windows seemed to make up a video screen. And on that screen was the face of an automaton and she was laughing.

The End. Or is it?

Acknowledgements.

I have to start by thanking my partner in weirdness, Anton. Life is never boring with you and your encouragement and advice have been invaluable in the writing of this book.

Thanks to my best friend, Jacky who diligently helped me through the process of writing this book by letting me send each new chapter. Your constant support and encouragement pushed me to keep on writing and I am eternally grateful.

Thanks also to my best friend, Jossy who encouraged and constantly asked about the progress of this book and has always been my wonderful, sparkly friend.

Thanks to my fantastic family, especially Mum, Lind, Aunty Jeannie, Alastair, Dad, Mary, Loki and Bao. Your love and support is the best kind of treasure. Your reading, cheerleading and interest in this book has been indispensible and much appreciated.

Thanks to my dear friend Di who has been so supportive offering help during these difficult times. Thanks for being there and being the best.

Also, thanks for my brilliant work family, Chris, Paula, Izzy,Lauren,Lisa, Graeme,Sal,Shirley,Sammy,Lee, Trace, Cee, Chloe, Sophie, Trev, James, Karen, Katie and Terri-Leigh. You always have my back and have encouraged me no end. I'm

really grateful. Thank you.
Inner photo courtesy of cottonbro@www.pexels.com

February 2021.

Printed in Great Britain
by Amazon